FOU_ _

ALBERT BAGSHOT

albertbagshot@gmail.com

Contents

1

HOLY MARY MOTHER OF GOD

'What he'll ask you to do is say a "Hail Mary" to prove it. Can you do that? No you can't. So I've written it down for you. Now you have to say it right, OK? So you'll have to learn it off by heart tonight. You don't do anything tonight except say the "Hail Mary" and you say it out loud to yourself so that when you do it tomorrow it's like you've been saying it since you were in your mother's womb and you're bored stiff saying it. OK? So have a go, let me hear you.

Mother of Mercy. It's like a donkey pulling a coffin. You've got to rattle it out. Don't think about it, you're not saying anything you're just showing your card OK? Try it again, twice as fast. Jesus it's still rubbish but you keep doing that all night non-stop and maybe it'll fall off your tongue like it should. You've got to get it down to eight seconds say, no more than nine. Remember you've got to rattle it off.

And here's the important bit now. When you get to the word "Jesus" just make it a bit longer. You can't get the whole thing out in one breath almost, so you almost take a breath after "Jesus". Try it.

Too long like you're saying separate words and you're not, it's just one long chant and you almost pause after "Jesus" but you don't, see?

And now here's the really crucial bit. When you say "Jesus" you nod your head, OK? You're supposed to bow but you've been doing it since birth so it's just a nod, like when you sneeze only not so big like. Try it.

God help us if you do it like that tomorrow you'll be in a box and I'll lose both me legs. That's all I can do to help you with all right?

When he asks you, you cock your head slightly on one side, stare at the corner of the ceiling and rattle it out like your order at the bar, you almost pause at "Jesus" and you give a little sneeze-like nod.

And so help me god I'll be praying to the Blessed Virgin for the both of us.'

,

2

A PICTURE OF BEAUTY

Mafeking Quimby stared at his reflection in the bathroom mirror before breakfast in his hotel room at the beginning of what he knew would be an exciting long weekend. He had organised a day or two off work at doctor's orders to enjoy a short stay in London taking in the pleasures of the galleries and museums. He had no particular itinery except to see a Bonnard that he knew was in one of the Bond street galleries.

But for now he was concentrating on waxing his moustache; a daily ritual given that his creation was a somewhat more tidy version of the Laughing Cavalier's. Nevertheless, the ends were necessarily waxed to form gentle upwardly formed points. He couldn't go as far as Poirot in sleeping with his upper lip in a hair-net but the consequence was the need of more readjustment every morning. The bottom of his moustache would need the merest trimming so as not to occlude his lip and a holistic view was taken of his face to cope with asymmetry, a characteristic of everyone's face but one that few people considered was ever a problem.

His journey to the Bond Street and Cork Street area was uneventful. Whilst on Curzon Street he took a quick perusal of George Trumper's window. It was too early in the day for any revellers of the type who would shout favourable comment on his moustache as if they were intimate friends, but he was aware of a few favourable glances and even of an envious one or two from young men not as yet capable of such accomplishment.

The exhibition in the gallery on Bond Street was proving popular, not exactly like a Blockbuster as the big exhibitions had become called, but there were enough people to prevent Mafeking from feeling pressured into close study of paintings that held no interest for him, nor from putting on an air of contemplating purchase of something quite beyond his means.

The Little Girl with Dog by Pierre Bonnard was everything that Mafeking had hoped for.

Sketchy in its forms as with all Bonnard's works, the painting was full of movement and light. The child's smile fleeting. This was one painting that Mafeking did not have to fake close study, he was engrossed, so engrossed that he had not noticed the group of three young women who were also admiring the work.

He almost brushed shoulders with them. He apologised to the tall blonde who was closest to him and admiring her legs made his second apology to her Rubensesque friend in a floral silk dress that said I am naked under this garment. But to the third of the companions he said nothing. He was speechless, staggered you might say. His jaw had literally dropped as he stared at her.

She was of medium height, on the slim side, what other women might describe as a "nice figure". She had dark wavy hair cut short and a pale complexion. Her face was pretty, some might go as far as to say beautiful but what made it unique, stunning even, was her well-groomed dark moustache.

All Mafeking could do was to mumble and make a hasty retreat to some other painting. He had no idea what painting it was nor could he even have described it to anyone asking the minute after he stood in front of it. He could focus neither his vision nor his mind and as others moved close to him in an attempt to see the art work he was occluding, he retreated to the cloakroom, where he fortunately found himself alone and could take stock of himself.

He stared into the washbowl mirror. His moustache was in perfect order. Well-groomed and well balanced with his face, his creation he had thought could not be bettered, but hers was so beautiful, so elegant in its femininity. Where his had a certain masculine robustness hers was silken looking, a full moustache no doubt, dressing her upper lip and lightly curling up at the ends hinting at mischief. He was touched by disbelief as well as admiration and had to see it and see her again.

Having regained his composure he went back out into the gallery. Several groups of people wandered around the Bonnard, but she was not there. There were other rooms within the gallery so he casually, as casually as possible under the circumstances, walked through into the next room with his eyes on the paintings but his attention on the viewers.

He caught sight of the tall blonde woman just entering the furthest room and he slowly made his way in that direction. He saw in the reflection of a painting behind glass the little group re-enter the room in which he stood. He dare not turn to look but he could see enough to confirm his first impressions.

The three young women separated as they wandered through the gallery and he kept his gaze on the one whose face mesmerised him. She slowly walked back to the Bonnard and he followed. He was aware that he was stalking her but he had to see her close again. He managed to approach both her and the Bonnard sideways like a crab, seemingly paying a great deal of attention to the empty wall space between paintings. But he found himself alone with her in front of the smiling young girl.

'It's sublime isn't it' she quietly said to him and her hand brushed against his. He dared look at her as he gave his agreement.

'Exquisite' was what he said admiring how her moustache rivalled his own for impeccable neatness, and the way she carried it without hint of the extraordinary. The guitar of Segovia playing a study by Fernando Sor, piped softly into the gallery and he took the unusual step of introducing himself.

'Fiorentina' she said in reply.

They awoke the following morning in each other's arms in his hotel bed. Fiorentina closed her eyes again in his embrace and he noticed how softly her moustache graced her upper lip, how beautifully symmetrical it was, how perfectly unruffled and calm it looked. It formed a gentle smile and so did her lips. Their lips met and they kissed for what seemed an hour.

It all seemed so natural, so smooth. Their conversation flowed easily, there was no awkwardness for either of them at finding themselves naked together. They half dressed and stared at each other, undressed and made love, and dressed again; made a little breakfast and without any consideration of whether to do anything else, they decided to stroll out to see the Bonnard again. They shared the bathroom and the bathroom mirror to groom their upper lips.

In Mafeking's mind this was idyllic. The perfect weekend was almost an insult as a description of how he felt and it seemed that Fiorentina had similar feelings. They were soon standing in front of the Bonnard and laughing at the dog that inhabited a bottom corner of so many of his paintings. How his jolly ears flapped, caught with a smudge of a brush stroke. But their attention was focussed on the little girl's smile. It was a smile expressed in her repose; the tilting backwards of her head to the adult viewer; a smile expressed in her lips; but above all it emanated from her eyes.

'You can see it in the eyes' said Fiorentina, 'You can always see it in the eyes'. Mafeking had to agree. 'Even 'though they are closed' said Fiorentina.

'We should see more', said Mafeking and they talked of seeing Bonnard's works together and their widespread locations; what sort of order they could see them in to facilitate maximising the number of paintings whilst minimising travel. Their plan was extensive, not confined to London nor Britain, but worldwide, so extensive that their continued love affair was never doubted.

The conversation flowed in and out of Bonnard's paintings and their life together. They were secure enough together for Fiorentina to mention the Laughing Cavalier and they both laughed. For the rest of the weekend, when not love-making they seemed to be laughing. Mafeking was sure his heart was pumping at twice its normal speed. He felt his vision was slightly blurred with the blood rushing through his eyes. He had the sensation of slightly floating. They both felt as if they had whirled around London the whole weekend.

Fiorentina lay relaxing on the bed half awake, half asleep. Mafeking sat in an armchair looking at her. When he looked at her clothed body he could not help admiring her graceful figure, yet when he looked at her face he was still consumed. The double beat of his heart almost stopped at the beautiful composition of her features.

The Bonnards had taken his attention from her but now back at his hotel his gaze was again magnetised to her facial hair. Like the smile on the face of Bonnard's little girl and Leonardo's Mona Lisa, Fiorentina's moustache was no accessory, it was the embodiment of her beauty. His heart was racing and stopping, racing and stopping. She opened her eyes briefly, smiled and closed them again.

It is probably true to say that Mafeking's mind was in turmoil but the next morning, when in front of the bathroom mirror Fiorentina casually mentioned the possibility of shaving off her moustache, he was lost for words. He probably made some non-comital comment but his thoughts had soared far from his bathroom and hotel.

He was back at the first instance of seeing her. He saw her in front of the Bonnard. He saw her on his bed, in his bed, close in his embrace. The cavalier was laughing at him. He tried to make her beauty complete without her moustache which was so beautiful, so graceful, elegant. So right. But he couldn't.

Mafeking had been stunned once more but this time it was painful as if he had been hit by a rock. He made as to go out to bring some nice bits of food for lunch and left feeling sweat under his arms and across his brow. He rushed out of his hotel turning left on the pavement only realising that the shops were in the opposite direction so retraced his steps almost running.

He worked at calming himself. 'I must keep calm, mustn't attract attention.' In the store which aimed at selling everything he made an attempt to collect the few items that anyone who had just arrived in a flat might want; wine, paracetamol, rat poison, bleach, dusters, strong polythene sacks.

Mafeking's thoughts were racing over the modus operandi and confused with remnants of the morning's conversations. 'Of course' he had said with as much conviction as he could muster, he loved her and not her moustache. But she was her moustache, wasn't she? Alcohol first, then paracetamol, then... He would always love her. It was her smile. Carry her to the bridge at midnight in a polythene sack. Once in the river it would look like suicide. The subtle curves, the soft silk impishly curled ends.

He blundered in through the front door. Calm, calm keep calm, he was repeating to himself, racing up the stairs. Composure. He lightly twirled the corners of his whiskers, grabbed hold of the wine bottle like a club and stumbled into his room. It was empty of all traces of Fiorentina except for a small note on his pillow, which read 'I saw it in your eyes.'

The following morning saw Mafeking poised pensively in front of the bathroom mirror, razor in hand.

3

HOW TO PAINT A PICASSO
OR
IT'S A DOG'S DINNER

'Feeling a little Cubist this morning aren't we. Now, where's that studio door key, what the hell does it look like? Ah, here we are. Now, let's see, twelve o'clock, not too early for a couple of glasses of Beaujolais Nouveau before we start.'

'So, a bit of a squiggle there, some big black eye lashes here on both eyes. Big pink nose in profile, too big, never mind. Oops, too much blue; can't have too much blue. Pablo, get out! Walkies later. How many times have I … God, there's the phone. Christ, I'm an artist not an answering service!'

'Hello … Ah, Crispin, yes I'm well, yes, tremendously busy, yes, so much new work; a new oeuvre, taking me into completely new territory. You're passing by. Today? God! No I said good, yes of course, extremely sellable, yes see you in an … ten minutes? Christ, no I said fine, it's a bad line. Wonderful.'

'Pablo what are you eating? Jesus Pablo, Christ, you've…get off it! Get off it. And for Christ's sake stop wiping your feet. The top corner. Where's the top corner? This, and Crispin coming and my one… and not to mention the potential money you stupid mutt, Out! Hell, five minutes to… to do what? It's a… God knows what it is now, and he'll be here in. Oh Jesus, the doorbell, he's here.'

'Crispin.'

'Damian.'

'Crispin. Yes of course come in, come in.'

'Damian.'

'Crispin. Yes come in, so busy just closed the studio, locked it even. You have to get out some time. Wanted to see the new work? Not quite dry yet. Yes I did say I've got lots, works in progress, not necessarily worth seeing yet. Yes a new direction. What direction? Er different from the last one. Drink? Yes of course you do, like a fish, no I said "like it fresh," from the vineyard, Beaujolais Nouveau. Yes sit down in there. Sorry about the dog hairs. Yes linen, picks them up terribly, yes, No! Don't go in there it's…'

'It's… brilliant Damian.'

'It's brilliant? Yes it's …'

'It's wild Damian.'

'Yes it's meant to be wild and brill…'

'It's so animal like.'

'Yes, it should be Crispin, I mean it's meant to be.'

'It's a bit ragged at the top.'

'Yes, ragged at the top. Do you… like ragged Crispin?'

'Oh, I like ragged, Damian, I like ragged, and the scratching, the scratching. Yes, you *have* used mud.'

'Yes mud.'

'And dog hairs. Oh, you are a humourist Damian, a humourist. But it's deep.'

'Deep, yes it's intentionally deep, very deep.'

'Not too deep.'

'No, not too deep Crispin, but expensive.'

'Where are the others? They're so sellable. I must see the others.'

'Others?'

'Yes you said there is a whole body of work.'

'Body?'

'Body.'

'It's, in, a state of...'

'State of?'

'State of drying.'

'State of drying?'

'Yes, the mud, that's the difficult bit. Has to be the right... dryness.'

'Tomorrow then Damian. I'll bring Theodore.'

'Theodore?'

'Yes, I'm sure Theodore will just love them. He has a buyer already for this stuff. Eric.'

'They're very expensive, and deep. Eric? Can you have a lot of money if you're called Eric?'

'A Russian. Russians will buy anything that's deep and expensive.'

'A Russian... Called Eric?'

'How many did you say, twenty, thirty?'

'Yes, that sort of number. You don't count when you're being inspired.'

'Tomorrow then. With Theodore, in the morning, all thirty?'

'Gees... Yes. Au revoir.'

***

'Pablo, for Christ's sake you've been sitting on that sofa all afternoon and all evening and all night. Christ I'm tired. Pablo, look I'm... *we* are producing great art here. It's always produced under stress. The great artist always has to fight stress and tiredness, Christ and I am tired.'

'Look Pablo I know I've told you not to come into the studio before but you can come in now. Come on little Pablo. Look there are thirty large sheets of expensive paper laid out on the floor for you to walk on. You can roll on it. Please roll on it. Christ I'm tired. Look just eat a bit of the corner, like this here... Come back you mutt! Get your muddy feet off the sofa and onto the paper you stupid... No you're not stupid Pablo. No, you're clever. Clever little Pablo come here. Come into the studio. Look Daddy will bring the paper out for you. Look there it is all laid out in the living room. Pablo! Stop cowering in the corner you stupid mutt and walk on the paper!'

'Paint, yes paint that's it. It must have been the smell of the paint you liked. Here goes then, big bulging eyes; nose in profile; big red triangle for the body; splash a bit of stuff here and there and everywhere. Look Pablo, daddy has put paint on the paper for you, on every one, Christ I'm tired. Jesus Pablo the sun is coming up and Crispin will be here soon, and Theodore, Christ Theodore will want to take some to show Eric the Russian with money.'

'Hell Pablo, don't just sit there, just do something. Do it now! Look I'll get down on all fours like you, come on Pablo. Please pretty Pablo, just chew a little corner, like this. Pablo show me how to chew, and scratch, wild animal like scratching and chewing. Mud, we need mud wiped about. Here Pablo I'll bring the paper to you. There's a good boy. No need to growl Pablo. Why don't you...Christ, the phone. They must be on their way.'

'Crispin, Crispin. Yes not too early no, been up a while, relaxing morning coffee on the balcony, you know, just to catch the morning sun coming up. What? Did you say Theodore's not coming? What? Eric's gone back to Russia.

I thought he was there already, he's Russian isn't he? Won't be coming back. Still, you could make it later now, as you're passing by. You're not coming. Wigan? Where the bloody hell is Wigan? Up in the North. Do they paint pictures up in the North Crispin?'

'Pablo! What the hell are you doing squatting on that paper? Crispin, Crispin I've got a whole new oeuvre for you to see. Crispin? Crispin!'

4

A LIFELONG FRIENDSHIP

I am sitting in the warmth of the Devon sun in August on the platform of Paignton railway station. I always take this route down to Dartmouth using the steam railway and ferry. And it is not the first time that I am thinking of a girl.

We met many years ago, it must be over fifty now and at that distance it is difficult to distinguish memory of fact from invention, especially I think with memories that are repeated. Like photocopies of photocopies, each successive one loses something and gains something. But something true also remains.

I was on holiday with my parents in Torquay, their favourite destination and we were staying with what you might say was our third generation of landlady, the first and second having retired and each passed us on to one of their friends, so we still visited them as old acquaintances. The landlady's husband was retired but had been harbour pilot and they lived in a small terraced house in the middle of Torquay.

The topography of Devon and Torquay in particular gives rise to interesting configurations of accommodation and our boarding house's cellar looked out at the back onto its terrace above single storeyed workshops overlooking a park. I remember the cellar had a most pleasing smell, the combination of damp washing and sea air.

The memory I am here thinking of feels like a Sunday and it was a short trip from Torquay to Paignton to visit our landlady's daughter and family. I remember precious little except that it was a pleasant afternoon. Everyone seemed happy, I recall that they appeared "nice people".

The weather must have been good because I remember spending the time outside on a large enclosed square of green grass, well cut. I played with their daughter, a young girl whose name has been lost to me for many years. I have no idea what we played at but I remember that she was sufficiently younger than me for it to be remarked that we had got on so well.

She was pretty and she may have been referred to as a "tomboy" but she stirred in me a feeling of what I can best describe as camaraderie. We made some sort of connection that I had not experienced before but I remember feeling that it was adult, civilised.

Although I must have been post pubescent, it was not a sexual thing. I may be exaggerating here but it was a different sort of communication to that which took place at home or in the school playground and I felt we were destined to continue our friendship.

The warmth of the afternoon ended, our parents made their pleasant goodbyes and our lives became separate once again, I don't remember trying to recall her name and it was lost to me quite soon. And though what she looked like was not a question I could answer, the memory of the afternoon and communion with her has persisted ever since. It often visits me with the same feeling of something unfinished, and each time the gulf in age between us shrinks.

Shortly after that particular holiday, my mother was reading a letter from our landlady telling of the sad news that her five year old granddaughter had died of a brain tumour.

5

IN CASO DI NEBBIA

A few moments of stunned silence surrounded everyone before the wild screaming and shouting erupted. The memory that would haunt Max for some time.

The day started for Max just like any other early June day on the road south east of Pisa. He was not worried by the road markings warning of fog, "in caso di nebbia". The sky was intense blue, the sun was up above the tops of the hills. Life couldn't get better thought Max as he dropped Maria off by the lakeside, dressed in Lycra and six months pregnant. He was heading as usual for breakfast at his favourite bar pasticceria, a kilometre of treacherous switchbacks further on. Enclosed in a clutch of hills which surrounded the small lake, the bar pasticceria was an unassuming rectangular building sitting above the lakeside on an eminence, fully glazed along the lakeside wall to take advantage of the view, it served freshly baked pastries and bread together with the best coffee in Italy.

Max parked his old cinquecento in one of the few remaining spaces at a slightly lower level in front of the bar and admired the view. The lake was linear and "V" shaped in plan. The bar was situated at the top right hand stroke of the "V", and the surrounding landscape was wooded hills apart from the odd olive grove and some recently arrived American agricultural plant or research unit which was situated out of sight from the bar at the top of the left hand stroke.

Local people had grumbled about this intrusion but greed, local politics and big hand-outs had secured its presence and once there it gave some local employment if not at the top level, which was reserved for the Americans in their Timberland, Ralph Lauren and Henri Lloyd.

The bar was filled with the usual group of Italians; men standing by the counter, dressed casually in well ironed shirts and chinos; each one eating the crisps and nuts provided gratis, whilst drinking or ordering an espresso. One or two Italian women were sitting on soft brown leather covered box seats at small tables placed along the window wall, smoking and drinking espresso and macchiato; and a couple of Germans were eyeing the pastries in the glass cabinet that was part of the long counter separating customers from the owners.

Signora Achille, whose villa now had a view of the American intrusion smouldered in the corner, waving a leaflet at Amelia behind the counter, muttering of GM and nanotechnology, which she struggled to pronounce and ascribing all ills of the world to 'foreigners', well within hearing of the two Germans.

The Americans were not in evidence at the bar that day which was the only portent of things to come but it hardly warranted comment on its own.

Of slightly more significance if anyone had been concerned to note, was the off the cuff remark by one of the two carrabinieri who had arrived for a quick espresso that all the American executives had left in a hurry for Pisa airport the previous night.

Max greeted Stefano the tall slim barista with a 'Salve' and indicating with his index finger that it was only one coffee he wanted that day, informed Stefano and the rest of the bar that Maria was not with him and was probably engaged in one of her usual health or fitness routines; probably walking around the lake. Even her absence was noted because Maria was a local girl and everyone knew she was heavily pregnant.

Max was English but he had been around long enough to speak the language and his marriage to Maria had ensured at least a superficial acceptance of him within the community.

Three broad over fed English fishermen arrived sweating, leaping out of their Range Rover filled with rods, nets, tents and boots, everything but fish. They crowded into the bar noisily and Max hastened to the other end of the counter away from the coffee machine towards the pastries to avoid their bluster and odour but he could still hear the complaining.

According to them the Italians had no idea how to stock and look after a lake, which was odd thought Max as the lake was a rich source of fish for the local restaurants. Apparently it smelled as well.

One of the men was insistent on scratching some green and blue sea dragon like creature tattooed on his bare left arm.

'It's going bloody foggy as well,' said one of the men loudly, assuming no one could understand him, 'and it's supposed to be bloody sunny here, this time of year. Three cappuccinos, love.'

If they were trying to be obnoxious, they were doing a good job, thought Max. But fog, that was really strange, and as he turned he thought he could detect some mist appearing on the lake from the leg that contained the American building.

Max was beginning to wonder about Maria down by the lakeside and for once wished that he could get a mobile signal here among the hills. The fog seemed to be advancing at an alarming rate. Max thought it wasn't so much like a cloud blowing across the lake but more as if it were growing, digesting the air in front of itself.

The conversations in the bar were becoming more animated and people were all beginning to look towards the lake. The three English left in a hurry shouting at each other. Max was sure that the tattooed arm was now bleeding slightly.

They sprayed a little gravel as they left the car park and turned down the road towards the lake, and the fog, the only route out from the valley.

Half a minute later there was the sound of a crash. The fog had now almost reached the bar and you could just see the cars in the car park.

One of the two carrabinieri rushed out, fading into the mist. The worried group in the bar now all faced the window wall hearing his car door open and a half word yelled as the emergency lights started to flash on and off through the mist. His companion threw a five euro note on the bar counter and rushed out, immediately being consumed by the dense white vapour.

No sound at all was heard from him beyond his first two steps on the gravel. The mist eddied around him seeming to take on some of his colour for a moment. The car emergency lights continued to pulse on and off through the fog.

A few moments of stunned silence occupied the bar before the wild screaming and shouting erupted.

Whether through routine or from some instinct Stefano immediately rushed to the well-sealed door and locked it, probably saving most if not all their lives.

As the noise in the bar subsided to that of a market like crowd, with half the group trying in vain to get signals on their mobiles, Stefano spoke to Max. Stefano had seen a small gap in the door seal and the wooden floor at that point seemed to be disintegrating. They rushed to plug the gap with some of the bar's cleaning cloths but the cotton ones rapidly crumbled as well. The synthetic cloths were untouched and the two of them stemmed the tiny flow of mist with some hastily gathered nylon fabric from behind the bar. Max noticed he had a nasty red scar down his left hand little finger and Stefano was scratching his wrist.

When all the attempts at phoning out for help or information had failed and the fog remained as a dense blanket around them, most of the group had settled into a defeated quiet.

They sat looking out in the direction of the carrabinieri's emergency lights as they continued to glow on and off accompanied by a low but continuous crackling or rasping sound. Gunter, one of the Germans was loudly berating his female partner in German.

'How much food do you have in here Stefano?' asked Max.

'Well, we would normally sell most of what we have baked in a day. You're not thinking this will last.'

'Are you confident it won't?' Asked Max.

'There's some more we could bake. Say a day and a half at normal rates, but most of it sweet. A couple of days bottles of water and milk. Plenty of coffee.'

'I know this is not going to make you popular Stefano, but do you think you could ration it. There are twelve of us here including you and your staff. If stretched to a real minimum, how many days could we last?'

'God, Max, that's a call. How would I know? Say four days, but I could be wildly out. I could estimate what we can let each have as a daily ration, liquids too and we could try to get people's...'

There was shouting and banging from the other end of the counter. Amelia was saying she didn't think it was possible, throwing a bunch of euros back across the counter at Gunter who owned an agriturismo estate up on the hill across the lake. He was already on his back on the floor, being beaten by two local youths, Mateo and Gianluigi, when Max leapt in to try pulling them off.

Everyone froze at the deafening sound of a gunshot. Max's ears were ringing violently still as he heard, as if from a distance, Gunter yelling 'You can't stop me.' Blood spluttering from his nose. 'This is a bar selling food.'

Stefano stood with a pistol in his hand at the far end of the counter where he had been with Max. Christ, where did he get that from thought Max as he looked around to see if anyone had a hole in them. Max asked the two youths to watch Gunter but not to harm him and went to speak to Stefano who was now accompanied by Amelia. Stefano said quietly that it was a blank but it had done the trick and it might be enough to keep people in check from now on. Amelia said Gunter wanted to buy all the food and drink in the bar for himself.

'OK, Gunter,' said Stefano, assuming some sort of authority, 'you can buy all the food in the bar, but as this is an emergency and we don't know how long it will last, the staff will ration it out to everyone in equal shares. After we get out, each person will owe you their portion of the cost. If they can't pay, then I will cough up.'

Rough justice of a sort, thought Max but it might be enough to keep a lid on people's tempers until we get out. Assuming we can get out.

It was by the clock, late evening, when Max found himself sitting on the floor in the corner behind the counter with Amelia. One of the effects of the blanket of fog was to make it dark in the bar even in the middle of the day, and it was consequently difficult to judge the passing of time by the usual passage of the sun.

Even the Italians among the group were now drinking cappuccino at all hours of the day. Amelia had been working since early morning which meant she had been up before the cocks were crowing in time to drive down to the bar, open up, get the ovens going and start serving coffee before Stefano, Francesca and Isabella arrived at 7.30. Despite the events of the day, she had been standing behind the counter, making brief visits to the kitchen in order to serve customers with whatever they wanted, until the Gunter event, and since then she had been sorting and storing everything edible.

Amelia, like Max was married, but as she leaned her head of long black hair against Max's shoulder he wondered if this was a sign of how far everyone was beginning to accept their fate and the fate of those outside. Amelia was clutching the small gold cross and chain around her neck as if a rosary and appeared to Max to be in silent prayer

Stefano's words brought little comfort to Max and Amelia as he quietly said 'The electricity has failed. Our small generator has started up. If we are to use our ovens we will have to do without light tonight.' Silence descended in the bar for the night.

Outside the rasping sound accompanied the slowing pulse of orange light from the direction of the carrabinieri car.

Hardly anyone slept through the night. One or two had slept for short intervals but the group as a whole were tired as dawn made the dark grey blanket outside just perceptibly lighter.

The heartbeat of light from the police car was in its last death throws and it made Max think that they were already down in numbers from the original small group.

Dawn brought something of a routine with the handing out of food from behind the counter; one slice of bread, one brioche, two pastaccini each, together with a glass of water and a cappuccino. The crisps and nuts that always graced the counter top were absent, but most were too weary to bother about this or the fact that they were no longer dressed in crease free clothes.

This is the rabbit in the car headlights thought Max. Several people had been lying on the floor and now took up box seats by tables, looking in rather than outwards as before. Almost everyone made their way to the WC without haste or complaint and the usual groups had clustered in mute conversation, and as the day wore on, the bar reluctantly continued to subside into some excuse for routine.

Small glasses of water were more or less freely available but espresso and its progeny were out and so was the usual activity that each one could focus their attention on rather than the big problem which was completely out of their control.

The only two who seemed not quite in acceptance of the situation were Signora Achille and Gunter; she continuing in the local dialect to blame foreigners in general and after his attempt at buying all their food Gunter himself; and he with his perfect grasp of both Italian and the local dialect feeling more justified in his attempt and glaring at her with a look that could freeze.

Max was thinking again of Maria and it must have been the case with most of the group, including Stefano that their attention had wandered to things outside, because the next thing that Max was aware of was Signora Achille screaming abuse at Gunter and Gunter returning this with threats to her, brandishing the gun that Stefano had used earlier.

Max was about to casually take the gun from him, knowing that it was loaded with blanks, when Gunter fired it and most of Signora Achille's face disappeared. The two youths, Mateo and Gianluigi, were on to him straight away and without hesitation had opened the door and quickly thrown him out.

He made no sound, but on sealing the door again with almost as much speed, the two were both red in the face and coughing blood. Their bare arms were bleeding too.

The rest of the day was occupied by hospital like activities. The German woman who had accompanied Gunter was clearly in a state of shock, trembling and sobbing, and despite the fact according to Amelia that she hated Gunter's attitude could now only cry out in German which no-one could understand. Signora Achille had died instantly.

Mateo and Gianluigi were less fortunate and were now the main occupation of the group. The painkillers that Amelia had found in her handbag did nothing to ease the pain of dissolving flesh. Even so, with time their screams had subsided to moans and by late evening as dark was almost total, first Mateo and then Gianluigi gave up. They were covered with black polythene bags.

No-one ate their evening food ration with any enthusiasm, and it was a silent group that gave up seating to lie down for another and maybe their last night.

As Max lay on his back he could hear the crackling and rasping. It was continuous but making less noise. Accompanying it was the faint sound of wind.

As the night wore on, the wind had increased and the fog was swirling around the building, rattling the long glazed wall. Stefano tapped Max's shoulder and pointed to the glass. 'If it doesn't hold it was nice knowing you.' He whispered as he climbed over Amelia and back to his place by the door. The wind continued to rise and rattle and Max seriously thought the glass would not hold as he drifted to sleep.

He was lying on his side on the floor in the stale air of the sealed bar, wracked with aches from another night without anything soft beneath him. His left arm was numb, spread out under Amelia's head, his right arm wrapped around her. She held him in tight embrace, gently snoring.

Max did not want consciousness and barely opened an eye to look up through the window wall to see a pre-dawn starlit sky, the strong wind had stopped, he slid back to sleep.

As dawn arrived, Max was the first to stir. A new world greeted him; an ugly lifeless world. He opened the door to the bar and the sharp fresh air stung the inside of his nose like frost. The landscape he hardly recognised.

What had been a view of extensive forest covered hills was stripped; not only of leaves or trees but soil even, every living organism.

Max realised there was only silence, not a bird in the sky, certainly no rustle of leaf nor animal roaming the ground; no sound of any vehicle from farm or road. The hills had been reduced to rock and mineral dust.

Others had now awoken and were standing silently behind him. The lake, which had taken on various colours depending on the weather and time of year, sometimes green with the troublesome algae, was now shining crystal clear in the sunlight.

Not a living organism in sight, thought Max, not even anything organic. The old timber news stand across the road had disappeared, all that remained was its galvanised steel sheet roof, now lying flat on the rocky ground. Amelia stood with her arm around his waist. She started to sob.

The little group stepped out and down as the ground was at least two feet lower now, any soil and humus having gone. Consumed thought Max.

They stumbled across what had been the car park over to the carrabinieri's car. On the way they saw on the rough ground the gun that had still been in Gunter's hand when he was ejected; one or two items from a uniform; a couple of badges, metal belt buckle Beretta automatic pistol. The driver's door was still open; the key was in the ignition. Again a few similar synthetic materials lay around; nylon underpants, a pair of synthetic soles from shoes, plastic ID card wallet, empty.

On the driver's seat, now stripped of its leather covering was a gold wedding ring. Max thought of Maria and the unborn child. He didn't want to think it but he knew now the child would never be born.

The small band of survivors, as one, looked East to the light green horizon as they walked westwards in hope, rather than in certainty, of a future.

6

TOO HOT TO HANDLE

As they wound their way along the half mile or so of bumpy track they could see smoke rising in the distance from the log cabin, long before the cabin itself came into sight. It was good to have the local sheriff's off-road Cherokee, their standard issue saloon would not have stood the test on these bumps nor would it have given them the look of police authority.

Elmsford thought the smoke a little suspicious as he swung the vehicle over the bumps and about the ruts, given that it was hot enough to drive with the windows open. Welkstein couldn't care less. Seemingly reading the map, he was silently reminiscing over the previous night's frolicking with Mavis.

'It's a big place to search. Hundreds of acres,' said Welkstein.

'What's his wife called?' replied Elmsford, putting an index finger in between his shirt collar and his damp neck in a vain attempt to cool down.

'Hey, take it easy on these humps. Gloria,' said Welkstein.

'How long she been missing, Welk?'

'Don't know for certain she is as yet do we? And lay off the Welk Elm.'

'Well let's see what this hillbilly has to say.' Said Elmsford.

They stopped the vehicle out front and walked up the two or three wooden steps to the open porch where Elmsford hammered on the door with as much authority as he could muster. The door was opened by the suspect dressed in old blue denim overalls, long sleeved lumberjack shirt and farmer's cap. He beamed a smile wide enough to close his eyes as he pulled the door to behind himself.

'Got to keep the heat in now the furnace is going. What can I do for you two smart fellas?'

'Someone in town said Gloria's gone missing, know anything Joe. Mind if I call you Joe?'

'Nope.'

'No what?' said Elmsford.

'No Sir,' said Joe and after a pause, 'I don't mind you callin' me Joe and I don't know nothing about Gloria missing.'

'Any chance we could come in?' said Welkstein wiping sweat off the back of his neck with his handkerchief.

'Sure, you cold out here too?' said Joe as he ushered them into the dimly lit hallway. The hallway itself was timber boarded, dark stained, dry, hot and cluttered, like a sauna being used to store old coats, boots and the like. They were pressed close together in the confined space and what it lacked in light it easily compensated for by odours. Holding his breath, Elmsford nodded to the room on their right, a replica of the hallway dump but at least a little larger allowing them space to breathe a diluted form of the gas.

'Any chance we can alter the heating in here?' asked Elmsford.

'You cold in here?' asked Joe.

'Any idea where Gloria is?' interjected Welkstein, trying to unbalance the suspect by applying tip number 17 from the "officers' interview technique handbook".

'No, I was thinking more like it was a bit hot.' Replied Elmsford.

'Well, I don't know.' Said Joe as both Welk and Elm hung on his words.

'You always keep it so hot in here?' asked Elmsford, taking his jacket off and loosening his tie.

'That's what she always grumbled about.' Said Joe.

Elmsford gave a knowing sidelong glance to Welkstein. 'You talk about her in the past, Joe. Does she not do it anymore?'

'Not as I know.'

'How come Joe?'

'She's gone.'

Elmsford noticed that Welkstein was reclining more and more to the horizontal and panting like a dog. 'Any chance we can turn the heat down Joe?'

'Well, so far as I know, she's with her sister, and no not really with the new furnace.'

'Where's the sister live Joe. You sure we can't turn it down?'

'Don't know, never was interested in any of the family and nope it won't turn down, built it myself.'

Elmsford had been concentrating on controlling the slight trickle in his armpit when Welkstein, who meanwhile had sloped off, maybe to look for air or something, called, his dry voice rasping out 'Hey Elm, come and see this down here in the cellar!'

'That's the Canadian "Elk Buster M2000" house heating furnace. Yep, built it myself. You can get a log the size of a coffin in there and it will turn it to a handful of ash.' Said Joe.

The furnace itself, a black horizontal cylinder about three feet diameter, stood head height. The front face had a door through which to feed the furnace and a rudimentary device to control air flow and thus the rate of combustion. The back, close up against the inner cellar wall, was a nightmare of pipes, taps, valves and connections. 'Can't stand to be cold.' Said Joe. 'We never saw eye to eye about that.'

The heat from the incinerator was overpowering even across the distance of the room, but this was where it was happening thought Welkstein, the source of the problem and its cure.

Elmsford dared to step towards it. 'You touch that mister and you won't even notice your finger's gone missing.' Said Joe. 'She's going full steam now.'

'You had this going long, Joe?' rasped Elmsford.

'No. Just fired her up this morning. Guessed you boys might be coming and thought you might like to see it working.'

'Well, I think we need to take a look in there.'

'Once she's going she's difficult to stop. This will run for two days now, 'till there's nothing left.' Said Joe with admiration and pride.

'Well, we sure need to look inside.' Said Welkstein.

'There's a little inspection window at the side here.' Joe pointed out after a minute's chin scratching.

Welkstein moved around to the side and Joe dashed to grab hold of a massive iron bar with a claw like end in his mighty fist. Welkstein lurched back causing a rush of sweat. 'We'll need this to try opening the window see.' He deftly placed the claw on a small thumb-plate topped turn-screw and wound it open. 'Now the thing is see I put this window in 'cause it was in the design but there's no way you can see inside 'cause of the heat that comes out.'

Elmsford sidled round but he could feel the heat as he moved his head closer to the laser-like beam of light that was firing out of the side of the beast. It was true, there was no way that he could place himself directly in line of the window without having his head blow torched off. But from the closest angle that he dared to manoeuvre he thought he could make out some long charred object that might have limbs. 'What you actually got in there Joe?'

'A big log and some branches. You can get a coff…'

'Yeh, yeh. We know. A coffin size log…' Said Elmsford, now with jacket off and a soaking shirt back. 'Anyway we have to stop this thing real quick and get it out. How do we close it down Joe?'

'Well the thing is…'

'Just tell us how to Joe.'

'See that thing poking out near the bottom there. Well, that controls air flow. Just slide that to the other end.'

'Got your iron bar Joe?' Welkstein asked as Joe was passing him the bar. He slid the poking out thing to the right. 'Ok Joe I'll have to tell you not to open this thing before we do. Ok?'

'Ok.' Said Joe as they were moving back across the cellar. 'But, if you want my opinion, you're best leaving the draft thing open, 'cause now it will run for best part of a week before you can get to open it, and if you're in a hurry like you said, then you're best leaving it as it was.'

Welkstein took the bar, walked back and slid the poking out thing to the left. 'We'll leave now Joe and be back with our forensics team. We need your keys to this cellar and we're going to put tape across the door with a seal on it. Ok?' Said Elmsford.

'If there's anything in that handful of ash they get, they will find it. They can do wonders these days you know Joe.'

'Don't be long.' Said Joe. 'When the fire's out I'll be gettin' cold.'

Two days later Elmsford and Welkstein returned in the Cherokee. The sheriff accompanied them this time in his own wagon. They were followed by forensics in their mobile unit - two large campers.

Forensics entered the cellar masked, goggled and dressed from head to toe in suits of some white inert fabric. Elm and Welk stood by them in the cellar dressed in suits, shirts and ties as before and sweating as before. Joe had on an extra woollen. Forensics did the cranking and turning with the iron bar and left with a handful of ash in a plastic zip-tied bag.

The posse left in a clutch in the order in which they came. Joe stood in the open porch watching them drive away in convoy from his door. They'll be mighty disappointed he thought watching their vehicles pound down the small humps in the long track.

7
SHEEP DROPPINGS

Tegg's Nose loomed above us as we trudged and tumbled down the walkers' path that, depending on time of year or the vagaries of the weather, was either a small sandstone bolder strewn gulley or a stream in full spate.

We were almost at the end of our six mile round trip, a weekend walk in the pleasant English countryside, blue sky dappled with small white clouds, bright sunlight, fields, dry stone walls, bold but restrained geological features and the colour green, so much lush greenery, a veritable Garden of Eden for both us and the animals inhabiting it. Fresh air raced across the fields chasing the cloud shadows and brushing the long grass. Warmth wrapped around us.

Straight ahead was an empty field, beyond that a field with black and white cows dotted about,

'Look, they're just like my farm animals' shouted Tim ecstatically.

'Yes and they look about the same size from here' one of us replied.

There were small lambs occasionally making tiny leaps in the air, free almost as birds on the wing. The field to our left contained more sheep, benign and content, like little clouds of soft white wool. Several old ewes spread themselves about the field, each with its small cluster of lambs, each mother tending her own little flock, a scene of pastoral bliss, all ruminating, simply living an idyllic life, plentiful food, no work, no effort, fresh air, huddled together in family harmony, no strife. Tranquillity was the word that sprang to mind.

We reached a junction in the path. To the right the path led upwards and would take us further afield. To the left the path led downwards, past a group of farm buildings and ultimately to our starting point and end, no choice really, especially as a dead sheep, apparently half eaten, lay in the gulley above us to the right.

'I wonder if the farmer knows?' Said Lucy.

We continued down the dry bed of the stream towards the farm. It consisted of an unremarkable collection of stone buildings and metal sheds that housed human and farm animals respectively, all in one great fuddle of collective habitation. We knocked on the farmhouse door and were met pleasantly and promptly.

'Hello there. Sorry to bother you, but we thought you might not know that there is a black sheep lying dead up your track.'

The door slammed on us immediately, followed from inside by a hoarse scream,

'Clear off, well away.'

We cleared off, surprised and feeling a little insulted but we could hardly be expected to know or believe what was going through farmer Eliot's mind on receiving our news.

It had all started a couple of weeks before our arrival at his door. The old ewe had appeared near the farmhouse for several days, standing there as if waiting for the opportunity to make contact with someone. If it had been human you would have thought it wanted a meeting, or it needed to talk about something.

It was an unassuming sheep in many ways. It was average. Its coat, neither pristine nor bedraggled, covered a rotund and robust body, like an item of small furniture, supported at all four corners. Its legs like furniture legs were skeletal and made for support and nothing else. Its teeth, regular as discoloured piano keys formed a mouth midway between a smile and a grin. It looked and was like most sheep unremarkable except for its lingering behaviour and a hint of belligerence and menace.

Eliot had not only noticed its visits to the farmhouse but had also noticed that this ewe made a point it seemed of coming up to him whenever he went into or near its field. And on each occasion it had struck up the same pose, four square on to him with a look in its eye that said go on then, don't just stand there dumb, say something.

But of course, as Eliot came to tell himself repeatedly over the course of several days, you don't talk to sheep because they are the ones who are dumb in both senses of the word, they don't understand and can't talk back. But sheep, as a rule, do not wait around mesmerising you with their look, like the ancient mariner catching the wedding guest. So against all logic, on the Sunday morning one week before our appearance, Eliot broke what he felt was becoming an uncomfortable silence.

'Well you're an odd one aren't you, hanging around like this. What do you want then?' He said.

'How about a little natter, replied the sheep.

Eliot almost fell out of his boots, if you can fall out of boots, but maybe anything was now possible. Talking to your dog, looking him in the eye as if he were your wife and receiving a bark in reply was one thing, but a sheep talking was only the stuff of dreams.

'Well now you've broken the silence' said the ewe 'we can get on with our little chit-chat' and, rushing into her speech without another word of explanation, 'I was up at the top of the field the other day. Yes, the top of the field, in the corner. Ah yes, our warm little corner, you know, the corner with the stone stile in the dry-stone wall, the one with three steps. Yes three steps, each of a solid piece of fine grit-stone, laid diagonally up the wall, the treads on the top sides of the stone slabs being somewhat slippery in winter but no problem at this time of year when it is dry, and sometimes you can lie under them out of the rain. Yes old boy, I was up in the corner with the lambs, two of mine suckling and two of their siblings, and we were just lying there, resting by the walls, as I said, in the corner where the top wall meets the one that runs up the field. Yes, what was I thinking about? Yes, I'm getting there, but just to finish with this. The corner makes such a wonderful place to just lie down and rest with the walls protecting from any winds and the nook being cosy facing towards the sun the walls warm up and with the ground sloping as well, facing the sun and with the soil being lighter up there which gets warm quickly, the whole place is just fine I was saying to myself. So anyway what was I saying? Oh yes, our little chit-chat. We need to talk about things, most important, most important, about food.'

Eliot didn't like the tone of this. His mind was muddled by this rambling but it had moved on swiftly from thinking about the impossibility of what was happening, to thoughts of the content of the conversation. This sounded too much like the opening gambit of a complaint, he thought.

Some time later in the week, in bed, Eliot was still thinking about this. The middle of the night was warm and deadly still with not a light from any source nor a sound from any animal. The room was as black as could ever be as he lay on his back in bed staring up into darkness. Eliot couldn't remember what exactly the ewe had opened the conversation about, he was still struck by the fact that there was one, but despite his diffidence and awkwardness – he was not a good conversationalist anyway – talk had proceeded over the last few days as it might between friendly farmer and farmhand or boss and labourer; natural enough conversation where one partner feels sufficiently superior and at ease to initiate first name salutations followed by inconsequential talk. The only difference here was that despite the fact that Eliot had lost his initial worry about the sheep going to complain, he couldn't get it out of his head that the ewe held the initiative.

It was Wednesday morning when conversation turned to discussion. The subject matter took a turn towards more serious topics. A few days earlier talk had occupied only a bit of Eliot's time as he got on with his routine of jobs but now it was starting to occupy and tax his brain too.

There were arguments raised in the sense of coherent sets of related ideas that made a point and he was at a loss for counter arguments. He was not good at conversation and even worse at either deep or wide thinking. He was a farmer and that meant to him that he simply farmed. To the outside world and those of his ilk who were less bothered with getting on *with* the job and more bothered about getting on *in* the job, he might have been referred to as a custodian of the English countryside; a vital force in shaping the landscape or an important element in maintaining the nation's wellbeing. But for Eliot it was much more simply I drive a tractor from this field to that; I fix this broken gatepost; I put these seeds in here and cut the crop that emerges.

Although the ewe had opened the dialogue with a statement about needing to discuss things this had not taken place until now when she threw into the conversation questions such as 'So, yes what was it I was thinking just now, a good question came to me just now, oh yes, what's the point of knowledge then? How much physics or geography do you know? Nothing at all I bet, so you could get rid of all that thinking stuff without missing a thing I bet.'

Eliot knew about things but he never contemplated the fact that he did, nor had he ever even given the word knowledge itself any thought. Consequently he could not summon any sensible reply. What the sheep said sounded right even though it felt wrong. Of course had he asked Bramble, his twelve year old daughter who was more schooled in these subjects, she would have told him about society and history and that it was knowledge of physics that had allowed his tractor to be built and a mixture of chemistry and geography that fuelled it. But Eliot's thoughts were more concerned with driving the tractor through the gate and fixing the broken gatepost and he would have been more comfortable with this than being tested by this sheep just like being back at school, and failing in the same way and being fixed by the steely eye of the teacher ewe.

The sheep went on 'And let me see, how many countries are there in the world?' and confusing physics with chemistry, 'how many elements are there in the periodic table? See, you've absolutely no idea, no idea I bet, and even if you had, what use would it be to you?' Eliot was desperately trying to picture a periodic table, and imagined something fancy in mahogany.

He just stood there looking at his dry rough hand with its dirt filled finger nails picking at the old red flaking paintwork of the tractor bonnet. It was easier for him to do this than to face the sheep and face its difficult arguments. As he picked and gazed into nowhere he could hear the sheep bleating on and could pretend to himself that he was listening but in reality he was attempting, it must be said without much effort, some mindless state of being, and it was in this mindless state the revelation came to him that for all its apparent knowledge, the sheep was ignorant of why it was here. Did he have it in him, he wondered, to broach the subject.

The conversation that Thursday morning turned towards religion and was the first of three conversations to take place over the same number of days, which with hindsight one might have seen as a slippery slope. Eliot was naturally unaware of any sense of there being a direction to dialogues let alone the fact that this one was downward.

'Ah yes, what was it I was going to say? Yes, of great importance to us all. It obviously has big consequences for you too. Yes, before I get to thinking too far in advance and start talking well into the story, well not a story but our thoughts on what we might do. Yes, so to start at the beginning. We, that's us sheep, we're thinking we might become Buddhists and we would affirm the unity of all living beings. We all possess the Buddha nature you know, and we all have the potential to become fully and perfectly enlightened. We don't regard you as being second class nor as being less privileged than us. We all continue to be reincarnated and not just as ourselves. We believe that we may be reborn as any living thing – even as humans. We are all one being so our fundamental principle for living is the prohibition of doing harm to or causing the death of any living thing. So the sheep dip is out.'

'Blimey! You can't just decide to believe in something just like that. You've got to...well believe in it, and anyway you'll get tick, then there'll be hell to pay.'

'Well what do we have to do before we start believing in something then? Anyway, encourage them elsewhere. We would be grateful if the ticks weren't around in our fields – most uncomfortable and inconsiderate of you. The wall at the top field is a bit dilapidated. I don't think it's unsafe yet but it would be unfortunate for anything to fall on one of us.'

'Ere, you'll be onto your animal rights next, you will.'

'Ah yes, did you know there's no such thing as animal rights? We are made to assert ourselves. It's our nature to be assertive in the animal world and animal rights are nothing to do with us anyway. They don't set any limitations on us but on you, they're to control your behaviour not ours. And the lambs, our children, yes they're ours, we care for them, you don't own them, they're ours. We own them.'

Eliot's loss of replies to these arguments forced him to try his wife as a source of information. He approached her about Buddhism at the dinner table, as casually as an ox on slippery ground. Her reply was as ruddy as her face. 'You're going daft you are. What you askin' about this 'ere religion stuff for' and mixing her metaphors, 'you're going addled, spending too much time with them there sheep.' But Eliot thought he might have a bit more luck in trying to find counter arguments with Bramble, his daughter, in persuading her to do her school homework projects on farm animals.

He could not help thinking over the day's conversation as he lay in bed that night and how the last thing the sheep had said sounded odd.

He owned the lambs, he had paid for the sheep in the first place, he had paid for their feed and the vets bills and everything else, but in a sense he could see the lambs obviously belonged to the ewes and rams, but for the ewe to say they owned them sounded downright wrong to him. Was this religion stuff about equality and caring for one another or was it about ownership and caring for a possession?

Eliot wasn't the only one to leave the day's conversation with something to contemplate. Somehow, amid the sheep's ramblings and Eliot's silences and stultified replies the subject of why the sheep were there was brought up.

It is often the fancy of people that they can see the thoughts of their pets or animals that they live close to. Eliot definitely thought the ewe went off in a mood.

The next morning Eliot went prepared for his meeting with the ewe. He had been thinking all night. 'If animals have rights then they also have duties' was his opening salvo.

'Well bless me, how do you know that?' said the ewe, seemingly having got over its mood. 'It sounds to me more like political rhetoric or management speak, not philosophy. Why should rights and duties be linked? Yes, why should they? Yes, if you have a right then you have a right. It's not dependant on being earned. That's privilege, the class system. And anyway we already have a strict class system. We heard about your class system so we adopted it and it works well. The better off families continue to prosper and keep their privileges.'

'But you don't have any wealth.' Said Eliot.

'Oh yes we do. It's based on wool, and the whiter the better. Those of us who have the best quality wool are favoured and get better treatment. This links it to birthright and so it goes on. Hierarchy and privilege are passed on within the family.'

'We've had this excellent idea. We better ones could become celebrities. You might think this is fantasy but we have heard of the possibility of genetic modification of ourselves. Yes, I hadn't seen it until now, bionic sheep. Yes, genetic modification so that our wool could be used as a substitute for tungsten wire in light bulbs. It's true. We hear it's on the internet. Of course, the potential benefits and limitations of this technology need to be properly evaluated, taking into account scientific data and community concerns. But the value of tungsten wire is fabulously more than wool. We could be rich. Just think how much we could get for the lambs if they were priced as tungsten wire. Just think, with genetic modification we would be able to increase yield and profitability as well.'

'And cloning too, yes, now there's something' enthused the ewe.

'You mean to ease childbirth and the like. I do all I can about that sort of thing without getting into these new chemical things' mustered Eliot.

'Oh forget that stuff' said the ewe, 'there are lots of possibilities there in cloning. Of course there was that damn Scot who got a name for herself for being cloned, but she never did anything. We could become really wealthy, not only that, we could protect it, keep it in the family so to speak. Just think, a whole dynasty. More than that, I would be my offspring. I continue therefore I am' it bleated.

But the reference was lost on Eliot who was scratching at the tractor and gazing at the landscape, with no inspiration forthcoming.

'Where d'you learn about these things then?' He said without thinking,

'We hear them in the fields. There's lots of interesting conversations and private conversations to hear as people walk through our fields. Nobody seems to think we can hear.'

Eliot didn't seem to hear either, as the sheep carried on.

'So the idea of the added value and uniqueness of producing tungsten wire by genetic modification and then cloning would seal our position. Yes and we could produce the lambs so cheaply. Yes, cloning particularly has attractions for a multochracy. Ah yes, I can see the future. I continue therefore I am, I continue therefore I am' it chattered as it wandered away.

It was early Saturday morning, the day before our arrival, and Eliot looked at his breakfast – sausages, eggs, bacon. It was all looking a bit too much like a family photograph album now. He'd never seen his breakfast as anything personal before. He'd never connected thoughts about personal preference for one animal above another with taste. How could he enjoy eating bacon from that detestable little pig with the black patch on its eye and its obnoxious way of limping about the farmyard or, more to the point, eating lamb from that damn ewe? As he lifted a fork full of bacon rasher to his mouth a rush of images of pigs' snouts fighting at his fork for the food came racing at him, trying to bite him. He dashed his fork down. He couldn't even fancy a mushroom.

He felt sick. The whole contents of his stomach felt alien to him now and he went out to work on the fields with sweat on his forehead feeling at the same time hungry yet too full.

Eliot heard the ewe chattering to itself on its way down the path. 'We want to eat, eat, eat, meat, meat, meat.'

The ewe grinned showing the dull pink meat of its gums. 'I want to eat meat because of its high food value and I want to eat lamb because it tastes best.' Caught unawares, Eliot made some vague objection but the ewe went on. 'Surely you can't expect me to believe that beef, or pork for god's sake, can taste better than spring lamb.' The ewe was following him about as he loaded feed onto the trailer and Eliot felt that its chattering teeth were far too close to his knees for comfort. 'Look we can work together on this' insisted the ewe 'you stop encouraging the rams to rape us and we go in for genetic modification and cloning. And we've had another idea. Inanition, you must have heard of it, failure to eat syndrome induced by stress. Well yes we can induce it in the lambs. We can stress them and save on winter feed. We get rid of the rams, clone lambs and stress them to death. It's just so economical. Give us some meat, we want to start eating meat right away, spring lamb it must be.'

Eliot carried on with his work in a mental muddle. 'Eat, eat, eat, kill the lambs, kill the lambs, meat, meat, meat' went rambling through his head all day.

Things were finally getting on top of him that Saturday evening after the ewe had left, when another altogether different sheep sidled up to him entering into a conversation of a quite different nature. This chap seemed to understand Eliot's position. He too felt the stress of living in these conditions of conflict and almost suggested that the sheep should accept their lot. 'We all have to die sometime. It's natural, we all die of something, I've been objecting all along to this conversation you've been having. It's pure fantasy' said the sheep as he turned to go.

Dusk was arriving rapidly and the warm red evening sky put the horizon of the field above the farmhouse into silhouette edged with the dark sentinel shapes of the flock. Eliot wondered if this lone one was depressed as he watched it shuffle its little black body back up the track to join the others in the top field.

Eliot would certainly be a sadder man the next morning but would he be any wiser?

8

FIVE FOUR THREE TWO ONE

We've all been there, none of us for real of course, but we've seen it in films or read about it in books or magazines and such like. Or we imagine it, seeing it in our mind's eye, having been told a story. It's death row.

We see what looks like a long corridor with a single door at the far end, which is the final and only exit, over which sits a clock to remind all of the passing of time.

Towards the far end of the corridor the walls appear to be solid steel but as they get nearer to one we see that they are made of steel bars, and as the spaces in between the bars open up nearer to us we can see that the steel bars make cages, divided from each other by other steel bar walls, and the cages are small and bare but for the essentials of sleeping and defecating and each one contains a human being.

This is South Virginia and all the prisoners are black, except for one week at the beginning of a new term of office for state governor, when one is white.

Some time back when the state legislature was reaffirming its belief in the death penalty it managed to pass a law requiring the newly elected governor to spend a week on death row within the first month of his or her first term of office.

There had been some discussion as to whether this should only apply to those governors who supported the death penalty, but since it was impossible to get to be governor of South Virginia without supporting the death penalty this amendment was never passed.

No one could remember quite how or why this law had appeared, but equally no one, especially no governor, had the courage or temerity or wit to question its existence. All simply complied either just making the best of it or trying to use it to gain a few brownie points somewhere.

Governor George Daley Jnr had lived a charmed existence. His father had created the biggest law firm in the state and George Jnr, his only son, had reaped the benefits since birth; a horse, well actually a choice of horses at their own ranch; smart cars; small yacht, 15 metres, you get the picture. Not that he had been lazy or had squandered family money. On the contrary, he had studied law, Ivy League and gone on to Harvard.

He worked hard and played hard because he liked it. His lifestyle fit him like a glove. He had come back home to work in the law firm, never wanting to leave and do other things, never wanting to take over and show the old man how to do it.

There was only one area where he might be said to have moved out of this comfortable bubble and outshone his father, and that was his marriage.

When it came to his marriage he had, you might say, hit the jackpot. Angela was stunningly beautiful, a southern bell, also Ivy League and Harvard, and as much in love with George Jnr as he was with her, but if this wasn't impressive enough, she was old wealth too and in such quantity as to impress even the billionaires of South Virginia.

George had come to be Governor on the usual law and order ticket for South Virginia, not in an extreme way but giving transgressors of the Law what he considered to be a firm but fair message; three strikes and you are out, with the nearest thing in his campaign to a rallying mantra being "Three, two, one."

During the campaign George had spoken briefly to colleagues about his possible term on death row but it was not high priority at campaign time. It was a brief and finite event anyhow.

The only advice he could remember anything of was from an old ex-governor friend who had told him something about appropriate clothing and not to get too close to the adjacent cage or its inmate, as it was all too easy for a strangle hold to take him by surprise. The inmate might find it fun to take someone else with him on his final journey.

But not to worry too much as probably he would be in the safest place possible, there being plenty of crazy people out there in South Virginia wanting to shoot someone and the ones incarcerated alongside him were the ones dumb enough to be caught and disarmed, and therefore relatively harmless.

He would be rudely reminded later of the clothing advice. And the crazies? Well…

Incarceration day or D Day as it was commonly referred to by staff in the Governor's office started just like any other for George, a five thirty rise; a shower; dressing without a mirror because his suit, shirt, tie and shoes were not only hand-made Italian but had been chosen for him and laid out ready by Angela whose taste could not be faulted, followed by the regular half hour meeting with his personal assistant to deal with pressing issues.

The only deviation from normality was that he would give the early morning round of golf a miss.

George was driven to the prison in his own specially adapted series six BMW by the deputy Governor, his running mate and long-time friend of Angela's. Their conversation, usually easy and spontaneous was understandably this morning a little stultified.

At the prison gates, the usual media scrum was there, not large, as this was hardly news of national importance, not news at all really. But space on the pages and in the airwaves had to be filled. Seeing them, George was glad he had not dressed down.

The sun was well up by this time and so was the temperature. Stepping out of the air conditioned car George was hit by the blast of hot air that reminded him that this prison was placed out here in the desert. Just in case.

There was a moment of handover when George passed with a handshake from freedom and civilisation to incarceration.

He hadn't time to make any kind of speech, even if he had wanted to, before a firm, not rough but firm, hand lowered his head through the solid door to the institution, which closed not loudly but firmly, and once inside a heavy pair of handcuffs shackled his wrists behind his back, and before he knew it another set were on his ankles, with a chain between the two sets.

A slight worry about the cuffs damaging his suit passed through his mind but he needn't have bothered.

'Is that really necessary?' George was in the process of asking, when the voice was already replying,

'No talking Sir!'

The prison guard's hand that had been on his head was now firmly guiding his arm as he shuffled from the door thirty meters or so across a sun-baked gravel courtyard towards the other side and another solid door.

George couldn't help thinking that if this court was where the inmates spent their time in the open, then they could make it prettier with some flower pots and maybe a bench or two and some paint on the walls to brighten it up a bit.

The guard lifted his key chain with his right hand whilst holding George with his left and turned three locks in the door, then tapped a number into a keypad mounted on the wall.

'You really don't need to hold me, I'm not going anywhere.'

'No talking, please.'

The guard ushered George into a small grey-coloured reception room with a steel topped counter to his right, on top of which was a clip-board and a folded orange coloured jump suit, and behind which stood another two guards already waiting.

It was dawning on George how vulnerable he was now and how different he looked. He had never regarded himself as small, he was reasonably well built and just over six foot in height, but the three men surrounding him now were all easily six foot six, several pounds heavier than himself, all of it muscle and black.

'Four three two one entering.' The guard who had brought George in said to the other two. George noticed that the one who wasn't holding the clip-board and pen was holding a small automatic across his chest, just in case, and the one who had brought him in was now standing behind him, close enough to feel his heat but out of his sight.

There was little small-talk at this point of George's experience. The guard with the clip-board politely told George to strip completely and to put on the jump-suit.

George was by now getting the picture so he gave no argument as the cuffs were taken off temporarily to allow him to do this. But he was surprised to find that his clothing and effects although logged on the clip-board, would be incinerated.

'Nobody coming here ever needs them again.' Was the reply to his raised eyebrows as he thought briefly of the cost of the hand-made suit and the Rolex remembering the ex-governor's comment about appropriate clothing.

He was informed that they had orders to treat all inmates equally without exception whilst in their custody. There were only two points of difference for him. By tradition he would be referred to as prisoner "four three two one" and not by his cell number as with all the other inmates. Oh, and after a week George would be released.

A different guard led him by the arm from this reception room out into the steel barred corridor of no return. He was led to the far end, shuffling, passed all the cells, each one containing a black face, some grinning, one or two spitting in his direction, most inquisitive but one or two just staring through him into the distance.

As they reached the end cell closest to the final exit, the guard unlocked the steel bar door, led George just inside and bent down to unlock the chains on his feet, and then his wrists. It was only at this point that George noticed another guard behind him with the automatic across his chest, just in case.

A week is a long time for a newcomer on death row. The state of South Virginia allowed visits to its prisons once every two weeks and if George had been more cautious in his choice of week of incarceration he could have been visited once. As it was, his stay in prison coincided with a period of no visits.

George had spent therefore the week alone; losing weight because he couldn't face eating what was passed off as food; bored, not having his usual routine meetings, golf and family life with Angela; uncomfortable, being dressed in the nylon jumpsuit, unwashed the whole week, sitting and lying on bolted down steel furniture on a bare concrete floor; embarrassed at doing all the private things in public so to speak; and afraid, very afraid, especially at night when he couldn't see anything, but he could hear plenty.

In short George was desperate to get out and today was, if he had counted correctly, his day of release.

George had been alert since the usual early morning wake up of a truncheon swiped along the corridor of steel bars, and he had expected early release. However, nothing had happened so far to alter the daily routine of existence on death row. No comment even.

At thirty seconds to twelve midday two guards walked down the corridor to prisoner four three two one. The first guard unlocked and entered George's cell. He told George to turn around whilst he fastened the cuffs on his wrists and ankles. The other guard stood back with an automatic held across his chest, just in case. They led George back, shuffling along the corridor.

Black faces looked out at him, some spat others gazed into the distance. In the reception room George saw a small but very expensive pile of folded clothes from home. He was told to strip and dress in these. He was then led out across the hot and dusty courtyard back to the main prison door. He did not think about making the courtyard any prettier.

On his exit from the prison doors he told himself to play down the hero, make it brief and get home for a decent shower.

He approached the small prepared dais with its obligatory radio and TV network microphones. He raised his hands and outstretched his arms a little as if to a multitude, despite there being few around but he knew it would look good on camera.

He began, 'It was a worthwhile and sobering experience I feel chastened even though I'd done nothing wrong.'

'Bullshit, you married the girl of my dreams' said the voice belonging to the finger on the trigger of the high powered rifle, 'five, four, three, two, one.'

A red rosette was emanating from the centre of the cross hairs on the breast pocket of George's white shirt before he collapsed back.

9

FOUR MEN

Our block of four houses built at the turn of the 19th century was home to four families in the nineteen fifties and sixties. The four houses had been built together but each pair was separated by a wall at the back forming two yards.

Our neighbours' yard was enclosed by a pair of outside toilets and store, making it somewhat more private and introvert than ours which was open. The advantage of ours was that it provided a view of the long back gardens followed by the allotments, then the recreation ground, the woods, a factory chimney and distant tree covered hills. It was working class but semi-rural, rustic.

The two yards each housed a pair of families, different in age and outlook. Our yard housed the older parents who might have been expected to exhibit the more introvert and conservative views, but Joan, Ann and I all went to college, yet Ian, Anthony, Jeffrey and David stayed within reach of their parents and their thinking.

Although there was plenty of the women wearing the trousers in our upbringings our destinies I think owed more to our fathers, the four men in two pairs.

The two men and fathers occupying the other yard shared the bond of age. They were I imagine about ten years younger than the two men in our yard, my father and Tom, his neighbour and mate. It would be a mistake however to assume that they were therefore the more active pair.

My abiding image of the two younger fathers is of them sitting with their wives on a small bench placed on an open shared entrance to the backs of the houses in between yard and garden from where, at a distance, they observed us coming and going.

On the other hand, Tom and my father re pointed houses, replaced gutters, laid new concrete floors, built garages and greenhouses, rebuilt and maintained car engines and bodywork, grew rooms full of flowers and pots full of vegetables in immaculately kept gardens, worked overtime and drove us on weekend picnics and to mid-week events. My father filled some of his spare time as a St John's ambulance brigade volunteer.

Religion, or its lack also gave a slight separation to the two yards. Tom and family were regular C of E church goers and even had a small harmonium in their front room. Dad was brought up Chapel but after marriage he followed mom's Catholic practices and narrowly escaped joining. He even reached the point of taking the collection tray round at Mass until in a sermon a ranting priest spat of his disgust at the ills of mixed marriages.

The younger families apparently had no religion which seemed to me to be characterised by the propensity for one of the wifes to use a two pound bag of sugar daily to light the fire and her being the first to acquire ITV with its adverts, which we kids all piled in to see.

The two younger men also shared the bond of a first name, Dennis, which conjured a certain youthfulness when placed against Tom, which more naturally went with the title uncle, and his mate Stan. Interestingly, the ages of Dennis L,

Dennis H, Tom and Stan didn't seem to be reflected in the ages of their offspring, although they each had two.

Jeffrey and David were as close to Michael and me as you could get though their father was younger by far than ours. The other Dennis's Anthony and Ian felt two generations younger than the rest of us kids, and Tom the oldest of all had Joan of my age and Ann, the youngest of all.

Surprisingly, the acquisition of cars separated the four men. As we were all working class the cars were old to start with and required constant maintenance. I think Tom and my father both had cars as a result of their willingness to work at this. Possession of the cars gave our yard a mobility which in a way presaged our social mobility.

The two yards and the bonds of name and age linked and separated the men in death as in life. The two younger men were both first to die. Dennis L who had lost his son Jeffrey at the age of about thirty due to cancer went not too long after in his fifties of the same disease. Dennis had been in the army and was a big Senior Service smoker.

Dennis H had been slightly disliked by my parents, having a reputation as lazy. Certainly with his blue beard and slim build he did more looking at than joining in at work that Tom and my father were involved in. But I think in retrospect he had a gentleness that was perhaps misinterpreted. Having experienced several bouts of unemployment his last job was in clearing out furnaces and it was in one of these that he met his frightful death when some kind of explosion took place showering him with white hot cinder. I recall that death was not instantaneous.

Tom, who in his retirement had moved away with Evelyn to be closer to Joan in the Lake District, was according to infrequent correspondences still laying brick paths and using the skills he learned on his way to being a bridge inspector for British Rail. But dad thought he was working too hard and that his increasing blindness together with the move away from his home community was making him lonely.

I think this may well have been true but it might also have been a reflection of my father's own thinking, which must have been the inevitable consequence of being a survivor. Tom died a few years after my mother.

During their later years together, mom and dad had taken up dancing, which kept them both fit and after mom's death it provided dad with a community of friends. Doreen was one of these who became very close. Doreen died some years later in circumstances which were easily preventable and my father never got over the fact that, as an ex St John's man, had he been there, and he had been a couple of hours earlier, her injury would have been of no consequence.

Dad himself died after a short stay in hospital for gall stones. He had these earlier in life and was it seems susceptible. But he was quite insistent on going into hospital to have an operation in his nineties regardless of the risks. Despite spending more time with us and really enjoying every little thing we organised he was wanting to die.

He was one of those people who effused on the bit of sight or hearing that remained rather than dwelling on the loss and he went into hospital with an enthusiasm for the convalescence with us after. However, he insisted on going home first of all for a couple of days after the operation and spent them gardening. He died in his sleep two days later.

10

SHE-DEVIL OF NAKED MADNESS

As a young copper he had assumed the bearers of tattoos would be full of regrets and embarrassment on reaching maturity, covered in ink. The busty mermaid surely wouldn't look quite so alluring on a wrinkled arm with deflated bicep neither would the watercolour rose wilting on a sagging buttock look quite so picturesque.

However, he had based this on the assumption that these people would be in a minority. The world had changed and this was clearly not the case now he realised, rattling the mouthpiece of his pipe on his teeth as he approached the mixed ward, hospital garments allowing views of flesh not usually encountered in the outside world.

Several bodies seemed dedicated to natural history; foliage was visible just appearing above the collar line having started its life as a simple ivy leaf on the ankle. Birds flew out of menageries that were merely a feather on the foot or a bee on the wrist. Goth and fantasy were everywhere.

The ill covering hospital garments looked run-down and worn-out but not quite as run-down and worn-out as the ward itself. 'This place has gone to the dogs.' Thorngrove said to himself. All public services were run-down, hence he was still working as a detective in his sixties, alone and without a partner, and here in a ward seemingly devoid of staff. 'Christ, the whole country's gone to the dogs.' He muttered.

He called to a young woman in a run-down uniform at the end of the corridor asking if the sister was available. Obviously the wrong question he said to himself as her glare heated the inside of the back of his head. Sisters, he remembered, were now gender-free charge nurses, although he couldn't help thinking that still sounded female.

Gender-free charge nurse Sledge walked towards him with the tight lips of a spinster. Thorngrove was still rattling the mouthpiece of his pipe on his teeth – he was towards the end of the fifth bar of the William Tell overture by Rossini.

'It's not lit,' he said as a greeting. 'Detective Chief Inspector John L Thorngrove,' he added by way of introduction.

'Charge nurse Seraphina Sledge,' she replied. 'Staff know me as the hammer,' she added by way of warning.

Hit me, hit me, said Thorngrove to himself. No, put your mind to the case you dirty sod and take your eyes off her starched white uniform and black stockings tight around her shapely calves and beautiful ankles and everything else and by god not a tattoo in sight.

He looked around the ward at the display of body art. He guessed that they could supply also a goodly handful of nuts and bolts; screws and nails; and pins and clips and other hardware from their ears, noses, eyebrows and other body parts.

Oh Christ I hope I don't have to poke around other body parts said Thorngrove to himself, this bloody arm is enough. He played three more bars of the William Tell overture as he looked at this bloody arm attached to the body lying on its back in bed – Tommy, the Major, McCree - local small-time drug dealer, wife beater, car thief, layabout, deceased.

He was parked at a gloomy end of the corridor with one or two other patients. Sledge leaned over McCree to adjust the cover placed over him, leaving only his left arm exposed. Her starched white uniform stretched tightly around her buttocks as she bent forward, Thorngrove lost his place. Was he on the sixth or the seventh bar? Christ he would have to start over again.

'Well?' Asked Sledge, straightening up and awaiting his reply to a question he had missed.

'Hmm, it remains to be seen.' He said, waking from his reverie and stumbling a reply.

'I take it you don't then.' She said, after a pause, her look suggesting he take a trip to the psychiatric ward.

Thorngrove examined the arm. Someone had very neatly taken a small rectangle of flesh from the forearm, presumably painfully before death as the heart had pumped out quite a bit of blood, ruining not only the bedsheet but also the worn out mattress beneath.

'This place is clearly run down or this little problem would have been dead and buried by bureaucracy already, without question,' he muttered to himself. Sledge had disappeared so Thorngrove felt obliged to enquire of a nearby patient.

On the other side of the corridor, partly covered by a sheet, was a large mound of a woman, recumbent and covered in the ubiquitous blue, red and green inks. He instinctively thought that something was missing and rapidly came to the conclusion that it was a fag from her mouth and chided himself for being just a little hypocritical.

As he walked over to her trolley, she took on the image of a Norwegian mountain landscape, lush green foliage on the lower slopes, capped by a snow white sheet, her arm resting by her side and covered in blue swirls a deep fjord. He played several bars of Edvard Grieg's In the Hall of the Mountain King before asking her if she had seen anything in the night; if anyone had been down the corridor or if she had heard anything strange, like a struggle or a shriek maybe.

He had no idea what she said in reply. He asked himself why a small rectangle, and what did it contain; why and how so neatly extracted?

It was now midday so he went to the hospital café for an English breakfast. The server passed him his laden plate with an arm that displayed several canines entwined. Thorngrove was Pavlovian if nothing else and, salivating, took his plate to the tune on his teeth of Walking the Dog by Rufus Thomas. He sat at a small table by the window. The café, no longer being part of the hospital, but a commercial enterprise encouraging all to enter, was patronised by several people with dogs.

Sledge entered with a hungry look on her face which instantly turned to disdain. Was it because of the dogs or himself? Thorngrove wondered.

She walked up to him with her lunch tray and sat down opposite him without asking or speaking. He was about to play the percussive introduction to Ravel's Bolero but thought better of it and lay down his pipe on the table. He immediately felt naked.

Sledge picked up her knife and with ease sliced through a rare steak. Thorngrove noticed she had a small rectangular badge with her name on it pinned to the breast pocket of her uniform.

'Did you ever see the Olympic performance by Torvil and Dean?' He asked.

'You don't like dogs I see.' She said after a pause, looking at her plate.

'The way they skated around each other, you would have thought they were lovers.' He said as the orchestral piece filled his head.

Sledge cut a morsel and tossed it onto the floor only for it to be devoured immediately. 'Are they predictable or unpredictable?' She asked.

Ah, very clever, thought Thorngrove. Dogs or lovers? Time to move on though, he thought, leaning back on his chair as his pipe rattled out the ominous Dance of the Knights by Prokofiev. 'Tell me.' He said, taking time off from the orchestral suite and, pointing the mouthpiece of his pipe vaguely in the direction of Sledge's breasts, 'Seraphina is too beautiful a name to be contained in a small rectangle. What name would you hate to see there instead?' He expected evasion or non-committal at least.

'Rufus.' She replied without hesitation, adding 'You still don't have any clue as to what this is about do you?'

He pointed the mouthpiece at himself as if to ask himself a question. And looking at the mouthpiece he said quietly without thinking, 'And what kind of person would have a dog called Rufus, I wonder?'

She stared across the table at him with eyes full of hatred and venom. He waved his pipe slightly as if it were an aerial trying to get a better signal and placing it in his mouth he mustered a random sample of Morse code on the molars. 'My guess,' he replied to his own question 'is probably some little shit of a drug dealer like McCree.'

'Do you want to take a final look at him?' she asked. Final? Thought Thorngrove.

Back in the corridor both McCree and the Norwegian landscape had been removed. A consultant smiled as he approached.

'Well, things are looking up,' said Thorngrove, seeing that bureaucracy was at last swinging into action, 'and how pleasant to see siblings working together in the interests of the country's health. Was it planned or did you just take the opportunity when McCree came in?'

Consultant placed his arm around Sledge's shoulder. The tip of a butterfly wing appeared at the nape of her neck under her collar. Thorngrove felt a twinge of disappointment.

'We should have been three, and Nicoletta would have been thirty yesterday, had it not been for his dog.' Said Sledge.

Thorngrove looked out of the corridor window towards the tall chimney issuing smoke from the hospital incinerator, placed the mouthpiece of his pipe to his teeth and lightly tapped the chorus of Ashes to Ashes by David Bowie, as a small tear appeared at the corner of his eye.

11

THE EYES OF PORTIA

It was not love at first sight.

My name is Arctosa Variana. I first saw Portia at some distance moving around what I regarded as my territory, the library. It was more fear than love and I knew that she was behind me even though her significance had not yet emerged.

Portia Fimbriata appeared. Her principal eyes looked forward, maybe she was browsing among books or more likely, she was hunting.

Ah, yes. She will jump all right with eyes that can discern more detail than any other. She will identify her prey and swiftly leap for the kill.

No web spinning here to ensnare her victim. No this will be capture and kill simultaneously. I could see her so clearly now.

Had she been merely human then I would have been able to see every detail of her spinal cord so vulnerable, and her legs so slender and frail.

Her gentle feet make their way over golden paths; gilt lettering on leather covers, tracing her way along letters and words that elude her. What bright path does she see?

She is getting closer and I see those legs again. Provocatively she rests them splayed open, tantalising yet telling, not the legs of a lover but a killer.

Oh, she almost saw me, but what…?

Another comes less careful. His name is Drassodes. He is grazing among the debris of skin and body parts that coat our world. So many times the books are handled and always rotting skin is deposited.

He is brave or careless for he cannot see with such focus as she and he sees her, yet not clearly, he concentrates on simultaneous visions.

He is on a forage and his eyes so beautifully created to look at the sun and describe for him his location and his way home knowing the celestial globe, but alas, there will be no return for him, Portia has already struck.

The hunter versus the gatherer, Homo erectus versus Neanderthal. The quick versus the dead.

But my beautiful Portia you hunt by sight yet you have leapt from philosophy to religion, an act of faith and maybe a step into darkness not light.

Come further down this dark canyon; make the journey from Christ to Ra. Come further to the limits of your vision, dare be tempted you are still hungry. I can sense your tendril legs nervously speculate.

How many times can you see me? Dare you trust the unresolved image; does the one glimpse contradict the other?

You turn toward me; we are face to face, our destinies seen so many times. I see you, you see me in so many ways, and you can see so finely the hair on the hair of a hair thin leg.

Come my darling come closer and darker. There is a place where light will fail you. Dare you approach beneath the Egyptian gods, close to the cities of the dead, past the eternal and beyond the beginning of time where, for you, there is neither light nor time yet the wolf can both see and spin?

Ah Portia, you taste elemental.

12

FAMILY MATTERS

Uncle Bert was a self-taught guitarist, painter and smoker of Park Drive. We always bought him Park Drive for Birthdays and Christmas.

He'd not only taught himself to play guitar but he transposed sheet music from the piano parts or other instruments that the stuff was written for and he'd play this stuff at Christmas and wheeze his way through the tunes.

The stress of getting the right note and sufficient air into his lungs at the same time created this almost impossible task that made his false teeth chomp and clatter like he was eating mints and emanated stress to the rest of us, so we would be sitting around him focussed on this task with stiff necks willing him on while he wheezed, teeth rattling like castanets over the guitar and we were just praying and wishing him to make the right note and the next breath and wishing to god he'd finish so we could get on with eating the chicken sandwiches and the chocolate rolls and sage and onion stuffing and trifle.

But he represented this thing which we didn't have a word for which we might now call culture but when he was around we didn't have a word for it. But anyway, he read books about ancient Egypt and he even had a modern glass fronted book case with about five books in it. At least two of them on Egypt.

And he had a bent-wood cantilever chair and three guitars, jazz style acoustic with strings on them so old and smoke deposited courtesy of Park Drive that you could hardly slide your fingers on them so they squeaked and whined whenever you or he tried to play them and he had watercolour paintings and an easel or two but I don't remember seeing much evidence of other painting equipment. I think he had moved on by the time I was around.

He worked in the steel works, like everybody did, but his job was in some god forsaken part of the process where the steel was like pickled and my mom always said it was his job that gave him such a crippling cough and was pickling his lungs and we all agreed and continued to buy him boxes and boxes of Park Drive.

The one thing he didn't have was a wife and his house was always cold. But he did have sisters, which meant I had aunties and I also had other uncles.

Not only that but I had three grandmas. I had one that was the matriarch she was mom's mom and also mom to all the other aunts and uncles. Then there was my dad's mom who was off to one side and somehow related to other folk my dad knew as brothers and sisters. Then there was grandma Northgate who was just grandma Northgate who brought my dad up and was a good woman and she lived in the same yard as Grandma O'Connor who was mom's mom. Auntie Flo also lived in the same yard.

So I had nine uncles and aunties courtesy of some apparently drunken Catholic shagger called O'Connor and one or two other shadows that dad knew called uncles and aunts.

Each of the O'Connors' aunts and uncles, except Nelly, Bert and Bill had on average a couple of kids so parties were crowded affairs and crowded by giants because I was the baby of the family as Bill once reminded me when I was eighteen.

If Bert was art and culture, then Bill was adventure and enigma. He was the one that got away to Canada, and did well, and then did badly in California and came back to do even worse in Sheffield and went away again to do badly again and then went into obscurity in Luton with a woman and then disappeared.

When he was doing badly in California my mom sent him an army cape that doubled as a ground sheet – Jesus.

Cousins Arthur and Tony lived in a prefab – lightweight and built like a sound box it was somewhat perverse that the hall should contain this beast of a harmonium, god knows how the floor supported it and maybe this fragile support was one of the reasons it must never be played.

What could be a greater symbol of frustration than this Lycos of a dog guarding the entrance to the home, met every day of your life, occupying far more than its fair share of the little entrance, pushing coats and shoes into left over spaces, standing there carved in dark mahogany with dozens of chapel hat-peg eyes on stalks each with the name of an orchestral instrument on it, a whole orchestra there in the hallway with carpeted pedals sized for some grotesque abominable monster and it must never be played. Always clean and polished, always left unlocked, the keyboard teeth teasing eager fingers, a daily lesson in 'thou shalt not'.

Perhaps they all stood around it singing hymns when we were not there. I don't think so.

My dad bought part of one of these prefabs when they were being pulled down to make a garage. We used it as a practice room for the rhythm group.

Some snout of a neighbour went and complained about the noise one summer when we had the doors open but by the time the police or whoever it was came we had finished and the ice cream man got done for his excessive jingle. Serves him right, the Mr Whippy stuff was shit.

13

SMALLTALK

We were made to talk, Charles Blather said to himself. He would talk naturally to others about the nature of the universe; the problems of other nations and the reasons why none of our bedrock institutions will work.

In fact he would talk about anything he knew nothing about. He would even talk to the police, doctors, teachers and people in complaints departments, in fact anyone who didn't believe him.

When we run out of people, He said to himself, we talk to other animals, on the streets out for a walk

'Oh isn't he lovely,

But mostly it's in the home with little discernible difference between human to human and human to animal.

'Pass the salt Dearie.'

'Go to your bowl Dearie.'

We talk to them in cages he said, and on swings.

'Who's a lovely boy then?'

And when we run out of animals we will talk to plants. Some people talk to plants in the wild, occasionally trees, but it tends mainly to be coaxing and praising; much more carrot than stick, as if to small children.

And when there are no people, nor any domestic pets and we have run out of plants then we can talk to inanimate objects especially to criticise perversity. We will talk to flat pack furniture; garage doors; bent nails and broken screws and burst pipes.

And when every known object, whether animal, vegetable or mineral has been conversed with, we will go on to the unknown and talk to gods, fairies and spirits of every description and some that defy, and we beg, flatter and curse depending on the results.

And when all entities known and unknown that we see have been exhausted we turn from the outer world to the inner. We talk to ourselves, occasionally with the aid of a photograph or a mirror.

'Jesus your arse is fat,' more often than not sub-vocalised.

Occasionally we talk to thin air with buds in our ears. It's a continuous babble running seamlessly from one incident to another the whole day long, until finally we fall into bed exhausted and unconscious and for some of us to just talk in our sleep.

14

IT'S A SCREAM FURNISHING A ROOM AROUND A PAINTING

The National Gallery of Norway and one of those chance encounters.

Edgar had been in the gallery shop purchasing a print of "The Scream" by his favourite painter.

Edvard Munch was Hildegard's favourite too and this was an anniversary present to them both, married for fifty three or fifty four years, he couldn't quite remember which.

He had spent time deliberating, up until the assistant had said the shop and gallery were closing, and eventually he had bought the most expensive one, mounted on board like the original and therefore the best print available.

He walked down the steps onto the pavement of Universitetsgata and crossed the road to Kaffebrenneriet, had a coffee and bought a few pastries to celebrate with back home.

It was getting dark on leaving, a little rain was in the wind so pulling up his collar Edgar hurried back across the road heading for Kristian Augustus Gate to catch the tram.

As he was passing the gallery he noticed a white van with rust around the hinges parked by the side of the road. A ladder was up against the wall of the gallery and there were tools lying around. The van door was open and workmen appeared to be shouting.

Leaning against the van, partly covered in a damp and dirty blanket and looking as though it was being thrown out was the same picture he had earlier purchased.

But there was something about this one that immediately appealed to Edgar and he swapped the two.

After all, this one was being thrown out, its bottom left-hand corner was standing in a small puddle, and he had duly paid for his print anyway, so he told himself, feeling only slightly guilty.

As he turned the corner onto to Kristian Augustus Gate a tram was arriving and he stepped onto it to the sound of tyres squealing as the workmen's van drove off.

****

It was two years since the second most famous image in art history had been stolen from the National Gallery of Norway and for many months little headway had been made in its recovery. But the slow machinery of police investigative procedures was leading the enquiry and everyone in the team closer to a group of rough local criminals and their equally rough hideout in the countryside a few kilometres to the east of Oslo; leading everyone in the team east that is except for Detective Inspector Tornlund who was trailing his own path as usual and flying west in the direction of Bergen.

At least I will get to see the apple blossom in Hardangerfjord, and who knows maybe something else, he said to himself as he looked down on the snow covered Hardangervida National Park, some twenty minutes before landing.

Fifty minutes to fly across the whole country and two and a half hours to drive a few kilometres back into the Hardangerfjord, but he loved this journey.

Steep wooded mountains, narrow valleys with waterfalls, deep lakes and fjords with round shouldered rocks at the water's edge like grey beached whales, the whole landscape decorated with falun red dwellings, like ripe rosy apples on a tree; the odd pine tree or silver birch growing out of a rocky crevice by the water; pre historic carvings on rocks if you knew where to look.

He drove to Torvikbygd and took the ferry to Jondal, the houses all white and wealthy, then along the fjord side road to Herand and up to the slightly elevated lake of Herandsvatnet.

Off the main road at the end of its own winding track, carefully placed facing west with a view of the lake in the foreground and the fjord in the background with its afternoon and evening sunlight sat the house.

Timber and traditional in form, its black colour nevertheless spoke of a designer making a statement.

On entering the room at Hildegard's request, Tornlund saw it from the side immediately but decided not to make anything of it.

Edgar invited him to sit by a low coffee table set diagonally to the right, opposite the door. Edgar sat opposite Tornlund with his back to the wall containing the door. Both men sat with bookshelves behind them.

As Tornlund faced Edgar he could see behind him book after book on psychoanalysis, Strindberg, suicide, Ibsen, tuberculosis. He dared not turn to see what was behind himself. From the corner of his eye to his right he could again see "The Scream".

The work had been placed on the brown wall between two chairs. He had seen that precise brown before in the forests somewhere when evening light had penetrated the canopy and the composting pine needles of the forest floor had sprung into life. He could smell it.

The two chairs, as sentinels, one on either side of the painting sat empty implying but not overstating human presence. They were Wishbone in oiled oak with paper cord seats by Hans Wegner.

A simple long rectangular rug by Måås-Fjetterström lay on the cherry wood parquet floor in between the chairs and cool grey northern daylight filtered in from the right.

The room was silent and it had a modernist feeling despite its verticality rather than horizontality. Tornlund coughed.

Edgar crossed his hands over his lap and said 'well...' Hildegard came in and placed a glass of Brunello on the table for Tornlund. He waited a moment or two then inhaling from the glass took a taste of the wine with closed eyes. After a little silence he coughed and asked Edgar 'How old would Christian be?'

'Fifty years old, if circumstances had allowed,' said Hildegard, standing at the door.

'Circumstances sometimes conspire.' Said Edgar.

'Sometimes to one's benefit,' said Tornlund.

'I didn't think at the time that I was doing anything wrong but mine was the first move.'

'And maybe that sets a direction, but directions can in some cases be reversed.'

Daylight had almost gone and Hildegard switched on Poul Henningsen light sources in three corners of the room.

'It's better sometimes if we can make a fresh start.' Said Tornlund, standing as the two turned to look at the picture.

'You might get the impression from the painting that this is a significant bridge or maybe even the only bridge in Norway. But every stream in Norway has a number of bridges and in Norway there are many streams.' Said Edgar as he put out his hand to shake.

'I will probably have to return.' Said Tornlund.

****

A few kilometres east of Oslo, the white van with rust appearing around the hinges was parked ten meters or so in front of the farmhouse with its back doors open. The two paintings were on the van floor, leaning against the inside close to the right hand door. They were draped in a dirty and damp looking blanket, which had not been removed as no-one felt expert enough.

The team was in the farmhouse awaiting the arrival of the curator of fine art from the National Gallery who would advise them of both the authenticity of the find and how to move it safely back home.

The curator was hurrying back from a conference in Sweden but had been delayed so the team had earlier sent someone out looking for sandwiches and were now all at the back of the house, in the kitchen, eating and drinking and wasting tax payers' money.

Tornlund pulled up slowly behind the van, put on latex gloves and, removing the bin liner from the back seat of his car, he walked over to the van, slid in one painting and slid out the other. He put the bin liner back in his car leaning against the back seat and took off his latex gloves.

As he entered the farmhouse kitchen, someone said 'sandwich?' to which he didn't reply but he poured himself a black coffee and sat down at the kitchen table with the rest of the team.

And so, to return to Herand a year later.

It was summer and the meadows had just been mowed. He got out of the car to the smell of freshly cut grass as Hildegard greeted him enthusiastically at the door. She lead him through into the brightly sun-lit kitchen dominated by a large window reminiscent of that by Carl Larsson, where Edgar poured them glasses of last year's cider, cooled.

They stood looking pleased as they both turned to Tornlund as if to say what do you think? Tornlund smiled and gave a slight nod.

They sat on IKEA Nordmyra chairs in beech and white, at the kitchen table which was covered in a sunflower print oilcloth.

"The Scream" hung happily on the wall above the table. Thornlund could see through the window the mountain tops still holding snow.

15

TED'S BALLS

One of the first things I remember about football in Wincobank is Ted's back, the back of a tall broad working-class bloke, a back clothed in the ubiquitous garment of the time. It hung from his rounded shoulders like a sheet lead surplice though steel would have been more appropriate and was finished around his calves by a slit in the centre.

This back had both shape and colour. The colour was one of those unnameable colours that is the result of ageing plus some special process. It would be described as a warm grey by the salesman from Weaver to Wearer but to the onlooker it hovered between khaki and steel impregnated oil. Regimentation and toil. A shining surface patina like grease and iron filings that was more than skin deep.

Not surprisingly and certainly almost not consciously to me as a boy, this back had not only shape and colour but smell. This too was the smell of toil, the smell of sweat and oil, the smell of Wincobank if one added pork from the butcher's.

Ted's back was every man's back; something to look up both at and to; something that got in the way (both literally and figuratively); something monumental, an edifice that would always be there. It was rooted in black boots and nondescript trousers and completed in the sky by a flat cap.

I remember Ted's back because it got in the way of my view of the pitch, though how it did so when we Wincobank supporters could have been counted on the fingers of only one pair of hands I will never know.

But Ted's back was more than this, it was the back that spoke power; it was the back that guarded the balls - a holy communion of vaguely spheroid bladders bunched together in a string net held tightly in Ted's pink left fist.

It must be remembered that whilst the skill of football today is in a poetic manipulation of the limbs around the act of shooting the ball arrow-straight or carefully calculated parabola at goal from anywhere up to the half way line, circa 1955 in Wincobank, Sheffield, the art, if it could be called an art (more appropriately labour) was to lift the ball off the sod.

But many things conspired against even this humble act. Boots themselves (a different kettle of fish from today's article) more closely resembled the animals from which they came and I'm sure retained something of the animal's mind and mischief in them.

Grass too, I am sure, was longer, wetter and more humpy. But none of these played as great a part in rendering football an inexact science and a futile art in Wincobank as the ball itself.

It is both an understatement and a tribute to late twentieth century leathercraft to say that balls are not what they used to be.

The ball in 1955 was much closer to its mediaeval ancestor than to its progeny of today. It consisted of a pig's bladder cum hot water bottle on the inside, blown up through a little thin but long willy like appendage inside a patchwork leather cover (rectangles not hexagons and pentagons as geodetic geometry had yet to be invented). The consistency of the outer cover was somewhere between tyre rubber and concrete.

Inflating the ball properly required something which most of us didn't possess. The skill was in having inflated the whole object, being able to tuck the little willy inside the outer leather through a slot a couple of inches long which was then laced up.

The problems were firstly not to let the bladder down whilst fumbling with the willy (best done outside in cold weather, preferably with bike oil on hands); secondly, not to puncture the bladder, and a special sharply pointed tool was usually used in lacing up just to make it that bit more difficult and thirdly, not to end up with a knot or bulge of laces that could take your eye out if you were fool enough to go for a header.

Ted, it must be said, was more than a master craftsman if judged against these criteria. In fact, Ted's balls elevated him to the level of fine artist and in many ways the balls would have been more appropriately located in the late twentieth century art gallery.

Although going by the same name and ostensibly being for the same purpose, each ball was different from the next. Although colours differed a little, shape was by far the most obvious difference - if the ancient Greeks had had these balls, geometry would never have been invented. No two were of the same size, not a single one was a sphere. They varied from the obvious egg to the subtly irregular spheroid - to say they varied from the size of a cricket ball to a beach ball would be an obvious exaggeration but it would be nearer to the impression they gave than to imagine them all equal.

But despite their differences, all Ted's balls shared two qualities which united them and set them apart from the common or garden ball of today.

In dry weather, the balls sounded a sharp ring of steel when kicked - the pain was equal to a smart smack from a real frost covered hollow ball of steel whether on the bare head (God forbid), bare limb (God forbid again) or leather clad foot.

"Toe-ending" with the capped boot was the least painful option but wildly inaccurate given the egg shaped ball.

Ted's virtuosity at pumping and lacing was quintessential. Pumped to a hardness beyond belief - no doubt Ted's great back had been put to good use - the balls almost floated if you dare kick them.

On the other hand, and it is truly the sinister hand, the Yang of Yin, when the balls were wet some reverse alchemy physicked them to lead, the miracle substance of Dubbin adding to the bond between ball and earth.

No longer so hard as when dry but now infinitely heavier and ominously darker, they became black holes whose only characteristics were to remain motionless and absorb energy.

You might wonder how one could get to know these tactile qualities of the balls with Ted's gaoler attitude to their keep, verbalised in such poetry as;

'Geroff 'm.'

'Keep thi fingers off,' and

'Whats tha think thaa doin?'

Sadly, the reason is we were allowed and even encouraged to act as retrievers for balls that had gone out of play.

'Ere get that!'

'Goo on then, bi sharp.'

This was no doubt seen as good schooling for aspiring young players. Unfortunately, as anyone who knows Sheffield will testify, there is no piece of land there bigger than half a football pitch that is not a hill. Wincobank is not the exception but the rule.

It was to be many years before I realised that the fact that balls always run down hill accelerating away from one was a physical and not a philosophical problem.

However, as a result of all this evangelically enthusiastic chasing plus maybe the fact that my dad was on the committee (I even remember him playing when someone didn't turn up - a much more courageous man than me at his age - must have been healthier too), I was given the opportunity, nay solemn duty of holding the balls, not touching them mind, but being handed the fist full of tightly gripped net in which they hung. Ted's steely eye saying all.

'Ere old them son.'

The Holy Grail in my grasp while Ted strode on to the pitch to administer surgery to some hapless lad attempting to lose his manhood before gaining it or worse still, crippled by the mere brushing of one of Ted's balls against his bare thigh.

Much of this took place on Saturdays, in the rarefied atmosphere elevated high above

Sheffield's surrounding smoke filled valleys on Concord Park, a steeply turfed conical hill containing about ten pitches with space for half of one on the top (now the province of those with little dimpled balls and metal sticks and too much time on their hands).

On Concord, several pitches laced closely together so that one stood, for an hour or so this one day of the week, shoulder to shoulder with supporters of teams on different pitches, facing the other way shouting different names and expletives at all the wrong times so that the whole park was a cacophony of shouts, ear splitting pea whistles and semaphore like signals, with balls flying in all directions, often at least two on a pitch.

On Sundays however, peace descended. Bowls, offered up by genuflecting elders in white, on a special altar called a crown green representing the hill, was clearly a necessary ritual of cleansing and atonement

Still, Concord was but a *tabla rasa*, a mere abstraction compared with the home ground in Maycock's field. Now a miserable little ghetto of rabbit hutches for the unemployed, at the height of Wincobank's footballing fortunes, the legendary and infamous Maycock's field was a rough assortment of bushes, grass hummocks, tracks, bare patches and a pair of goal posts on the fringe of the urban village of steel that was Wincobank.

Maycock was a butcher with a Ted style coat, brown leather gaiters and a false leg (There is something of black humour in having both the trade of savage amputation and the result of it).

The butcher's shop-cum-house was right by the entrance to the field which was a gated grassy track. I don't remember it ever being closed. But I do remember that for some reason one always tried to gain inconspicuous entry into the field, a carefully chosen moment possibly when a customer was being served (the shop door was always open to view... and smell) otherwise;

'What thaa doin theer?' (sally from shop door)

'Am wi mi dad' (half truth)

'Oh aye....' (disbelief)

Entry gained, along the short track (a few yards), through a gaggle of white geese (look out at Christmas), over hummocks of gold flecked grass and onto the lush meadow of the pitch.

Words are interesting and both field and pitch poetically describe the characteristics of what was home for Wincobank and Blackburn F C known colloquially as The Bank.

Field describes the semi natural, rural characteristic of the surface - rough in parts, dug up, limed, a place of livelihood not leisure (esp. for pasture or tillage).

Pitch - in the Pocket Oxford Dictionary (I could never afford a bigger one) means to throw, fling or plunge and this is mercilessly what the pitch did. By its Eiger like gradient it attempted to throw man and ball off at every turn - goal keepers clung to the posts whenever the game allowed and sometimes even when not.

Kicking uphill on a wet day (what other days were there?) and you were lucky to move the lead bladder from the centre spot to the centre circle. Attempts at greater feats were known but so were hernias.

Kicking downhill on a frosty or sunny dry as a bone day (what other days were there when kicking downhill) was equally impossible. Bullet straight horizontal shots from outside the penalty area though few and far between were bound to clear the top of the goal posts due to the excessive gradient.

Furthermore, ball, boot and beer ensured that most shots had curved trajectories, mainly in the upward direction, but generally anywhere downhill but goal.

A Saturday afternoon match was therefore inevitably a chaotic affair.

A motley assemblage of around eleven poor souls hacked and coughed, fell and spat their way about the pitch, winning as many, if not more, games than they lost (the opposition was usually an equally hapless lot and even sometimes unprepared, having the misfortune of half their home pitch being on the level). They were cajoled and "encouraged" by the calls of the half dozen faithless supporters and the odd dog.

'C'mon the bank' (me).

'Ger in theer. Gerrit in' net' (dad).

'Stop yer pussy futtin' abaat' (Ted).

'C'mon the bank' (me).

'Goo on, kick the bloody thing' (dad).

All this including the returns of Saturday dinner (with Yorkshire Relish), whelps and farts from the beery guts on the pitch, fits of coughing (especially for the first ten minutes) from the smokers (everybody) while both teams straight from the works (via the Engineers Arms and others) in billowing shorts sliced at each other with leather and nail studs, trudged uphill, fell downhill, spat, coughed and toe-ended their way to Australia, sweating beads of pork dripping and for what?

Fortune was certainly not in the offering, but while on the pitch and for the rest of the day if they won well, or lost badly, they were heroes of a sort.

But I suppose, most of all, their task in life was to give poetic purpose to the skills of the likes of Ted.

16
DON'T QUOTE ME

'Frankly, my dear, I don't give a damn,' Limpet muttered to himself as he put the last spade-full of soil onto the low mound at the bottom of the garden, four foot under which lay the dead body of his wife Marion. She had nagged, but no more than any other wife who did nothing but wanted everything. No, he had killed her... well, just because... he couldn't remember.

'Now,' he said to himself in his best Greta Garbo accent 'I want to be alone.' But it was not to be. Dragging the large plastic sack down the garden at midnight and digging a large hole in the lawn was not without its unique sounds, sounds that would attract the curiosity of insomniac neighbours and in his case all his neighbours. It was a wonder that he did not feel the draught of all the curtains wafting.

Kit Holden Limpet to give him his full name, was now in the interview room, humming to himself, 'Yesterday, all my troubles seemed so far away.'

'You need a drink mate, tea or coffee?' said a head on top of a uniform appearing around the door.

'All you need is love,' Limpet mused before choosing the former as he let his gaze wander around the room trying to understand his place in the universe. 'Listen' he said to himself, 'It's a tough universe. There's all sorts of people and things trying to do you, kill you, rip you off, everything. If you're going to survive out there, you've really got to know where your towel is.'

'Name, just for the record,' said the plain clothes voice on the opposite side of the coffee table.

'Don't tell him Pike!'

'What? You joking? This is a serious matter Sir.'

'I don't mind if you don't like my manners. I don't like 'em myself.'

'Listen Sir, we just need to establish a few facts here. We are concerned with the whereabouts of your wife and would like to know if you know anything about it.'

Limpet smiled as he pictured himself in front of the motel, looking up at the tall windows under the gaunt overhanging eaves. Could he see her already behind the shower curtain?

'Ok Sir, let's try something else. Can you tell us what you were doing, what you were wearing and where you were last night?'

He took a deep breath, leaned well back on his chair so far it was on its back legs. He stared at the ceiling, as if he were about to exhale slowly, emptying his lungs from a cigarette, 'I tried smoking and wearing a fedora hat. I see myself always in a lonely street, in lonely rooms, puzzled but never quite defeated.'

'Just let me get this straight Sir,' said the plain clothes. 'By the way are you quite feeling yourself?'

'I am just going outside and may be some time.'

'I'm sorry Sir but you can't just leave.'

'I'll be back.'

'I'm afraid we can't just let you go at the moment Sir, just in case you should, as it were, fly away.'

'I am no bird; and no net ensnares me; I am a free human being with an independent will,' he said as he rushed to the door.

Amid the clatter of chair legs and the rustle of blue surge and bullet proof vests, and the smell of sweat under armpits, he was heard to chirp 'Float like a butterfly, sting like a bee' as he flailed his fists around wildly.

He awoke in a hospital bed, bandaged around his head and one eye, his arm in plaster set at a right angle and his leg in plaster raised off the bed at the foot supported by a system of pulleys. He was singing softly to himself 'I've got you under my skin.'

'What's that you said?' asked the sister in charge.

'I'm the singing detective. Didn't you know?'

'I don't know about that Love, but there's a detective coming to see you this…well any time now.'

'The little grey cells will have to be working overtime then.'

'Well you do sound confused, you sure you can see him?'

'The trouble you can get into, just 'cause you want 5, 000 bucks.' He muttered.

'Did you say ducks?'

Sister Sledge heard the door buzzer and left his room, locking the door behind her. She walked down the short beige-coloured corridor to the outer unit door and peered through the small square Georgian-wired glass viewing window. She made gesticulating actions with her arms and mouthed words that were accompanied by loud breaths peppered with tiny word like sounds.

The face that occupied the whole of the window on view to her stared uncomprehending, but slowly raised a small card in a plastic wallet. It showed a thumb-print sized picture of a face that approximated the one in the window, but importantly it contained the word "Police".

Sister Sledge pressed several buttons on the door lock and the face entered in plain clothes.

'I wouldn't say he's quite feeling himself at the moment,' she said turning away and walking back to his room in a crisp starched uniform manner that indicated she should be followed.

'God I love those hips' said Plain Clothes to himself.

They entered Kit Holden Limpet's room to find him out of bed and, despite being encumbered by plasterwork, trying to heave off the floor the plumbed-in vanity unit, wash bowl and all. 'I must be crazy to be in a loony bin like this.'

'Come on now Sir' said Plain Clothes, 'Let's have you back in bed.'

'We'll just tuck you in, nice and comfy, and get that arm and leg sorted,' said sister Sledge.

'Asta la vista baby.'

'I think I might leave my talk with him 'till a little later,' Plain Clothes said to Sledge, making the latest in a long line of errors of judgement in his career.

Like so many situations where every possible scenario seems to have been anticipated and catered for, life once again just reveals its creative capacity for "slippage", a crack to open between the tectonic plates of daily mediocracy.

The secure unit rules, as byzantine as they were, just weren't quite capable of closing off the niche that opened as a result of the combined actions of the fire brigade arriving the following day to undertake the annual check on the alarm systems; Sledge having one hell of a hangover and calling in sick; the plumber arriving to fix the now leaking vanity unit and Luther Weildor, across the corridor, having one of his Napoleon days and bellowing that he was being poisoned by the paint on the walls of his room.

Whilst just about everyone available in the institution was struggling in one way or another with the howling and general malarkey of Luther Weildor, whose name by the way is an anagram of "I rule the world", Kit Holden Limpet, whose name you may wish to know is an anagram of "Don't tell him Pike", was slipping, well let's say hobbling out of the ward, unit and building.

'All for one and one for all,' he shouted as he launched himself straight for the dense shrubbery of the Laurus nobilis that pervaded the landscaped grounds of the hospital and dug deep into the evergreen to evade the eyes of the inevitable search party that was to follow. A perfectly executed escape you could say, except for the fact that his large white-plaster covered leg waved atop of the bush like a flag of surrender.

A little while later, Limpet was sitting in the interview room, still plastered and bandaged with a few extra bandages over the scratches from the shrubbery and his painful extrication from it. Plain Clothes sat opposite him stroking his chin with his left hand, his elbow on the hard table in between them.

I'll play him at his own game. Plain Clothes' brilliant idea came to him, he imagined like a light being switched on. Alas, it was more a switch being thrown with no bulb in the socket.

'Well, all's well that ends well,' said Limpet.

'Everyone is wise until he speaks,' replied P. C.

'A lie told often enough becomes the truth.' Limpet

'Don't put all your eggs in one basket.' P. C.

'But it's the truth even if it didn't happen.'

'Actions speak louder than words.' P.C. trying to keep a line on this.

'All generalisations are dangerous, even this one.'

'Be yourself; everyone else is already taken.' P.C. losing it.

'…if you can't handle me at my worst, then you sure as hell don't deserve me at my best.'

'If you tell the truth, you don't have to remember anything.' One last shot.

'A long time ago in a galaxy far, far away….'

'Oh hell, where is this guy?' said P. C. to himself in a low and definitely resigned voice. Raising himself out of his chair whilst wiping the sweat from his brow he grumbled 'I'll just have to get the boss.'

Three cups of tea later, as the red orb of the sun is setting outside and a secure warm glow is embalming him inside, Kit Holden Limpet sits facing and staring at the boss but his gaze is at some distant point in the universe, far, far away, as he listens to the words of Mao – 'To read too many books is harmful' he hears.

'So,' repeats inspector Thorngrove after a suitable interval, rattling his yellowed piano-key teeth with the mouthpiece of his pipe. 'Just tell us in your own words what happened.'

17

A SHOT IN THE ARM

Cutting from an article, author anon, the Newcastle Sentinel, 4th January 1996

A twenty nine year old man was found shot dead in a ditch close to the Crown Hotel last night.

The young man was Captain John Lloyd who had recently returned from active service in Northern Ireland.

Police say he was drinking on his own in the hotel earlier in the evening without incident. They are treating the death as murder and, as at present it appears motiveless, they are appealing for witnesses.

Captain Lloyd's great grandfather was decorated posthumously for gallantry in the First World War...

A text from Stewart Eward to Declan Briggs Sunderland, 29th December 1995

Poss the ans 2 yr probs. I got an AK frm bsnia. U ought to do smthing with it

Extract from a text, Declan Briggs to Stewart Eward, Newcastle, 27th December 1995

…cant believe smug little bugger Lloyd sits in here grinning and downing his pint… cu here later…

Extract from a text, Stewart Eward to Declan Briggs, Sunderland, 26th December 1995

…seen proof that your gt grndad was shot by his CO who got a gong 4 his work - name was Lloyd, seen the grndson drnking in the crown - the bastd toffs are still on top…

Extract from a letter, Alan Jones to Stewart Eward, 6th June 1994

...interesting to make contact w those who had grandfathers or great grandfathers in the trenches in the Somme.

I have little interest myself in the events of WW1 or any war for that matter but I have a bundle of letters that were written by my grandfather Thomas Jones about that time.

I haven't read them all myself but if there is anything in them of use to you in constructing your website, whatever that is, then you are free to use them. I have posted them today and would be grateful if you would return them after you have read or copied them.

Ps I'm sure you are right about some of our men being shot by their officers

Extract from a letter, Private Thomas Jones to his father, 12th August 1920

…I am finally out of the whole bloody mess. I don't expect I will be able to get a job, all the jobs will have gone to the toffs. I'm sick of the whole bloody lot of them, Germans and our lot.

I know you won't believe me but I saw my best mate Briggs taken out to the woods and shot in the back by our own sergeant - Eward, a real bastard – though on orders from the captain, I saw them talking about it and the captain pointing to the woods.

Where's the justice…

Extract from the diary of Captain John Lloyd, the Somme, 1st January 1916

…Yesterday saw young Private Briggs finally succumb to shell shock. He was panicking to such an extent that he was becoming a real danger to us all, especially to himself.

We are going out of the trenches and over the top in a few days and I fear he will not make it. I am still under instructions to shoot any who refuse to advance.

I have told Sergeant Eward to get Lloyd drunk and to keep him drunk for a couple of days to see if he can snap out of it but I doubt he can…

Extract from last diary entry of Captain John Lloyd, the Somme, 4th January 1916

…Briggs still as bad as ever. Told Eward to take the lad out, into the copse behind us and put a bullet clean through his left arm, making sure there is no bullet left in the arm and to send him back home wounded in action.

Eward is a bit sadistic and I am not sure I can trust him, he's an old regular, but there are so few men now I have no option…

THE END

albertbagshot@gmail.com

Printed in Poland
by Amazon Fulfillment
Poland Sp. z o.o., Wrocław